the celibacy club

stories by **janice eidus**

**city lights
san francisco**

Cover design: Rex Ray
Book design: Robert Sharrard
Typography: Harvest Graphics
Author photo: Star Black

Library of Congress Cataloging-in-Publication Data

Eidus, Janice.
    The celibacy club.   #34989966
        p.   cm.
    ISBN 0-87286-322-0
    I. Title.
    PS3555.I38C4   1996
    813'.54 — dc20   96-9671
                                                   CIP

City Lights Books are available to bookstores through our
primary distributor: Subterranean Company. P.O. Box 160,
265 S. 5th St., Monroe, OR 97456. 541-847-5274. Toll-free
orders 800-274-7826. Fax 541-847-6018. Our books are also
available through library jobbers and regional distributors.
For personal orders and catalogs, please write to City Lights
Books, 261 Columbus Avenue, San Francisco CA 94133.

CITY LIGHTS BOOKS are edited by Lawrence Ferlinghetti
and Nancy J. Peters and published at the City Lights Bookstore,
261 Columbus Avenue, San Francisco, CA 94133.

This book, like the others, is for John.

ACKNOWLEDGMENTS

I would like to thank the artists' colonies where I wrote many of these stories: the Corporation of Yaddo; the MacDowell Colony; the Virginia Center for the Creative Arts; and the Ragdale Foundation.

Also, I would like to express my gratitude to the editors of the magazines and anthologies in which some of these stories first appeared: William Abrahams, Richard Peabody, Lucinda Ebersole, M. Mark, Christine Iwanicki, Alexander Laurence, Matt Jaffe, Michael Hathaway, Judith Emlyn Johnson, Peggy Woods, Greg Boyd, Doug Rice, Alison S. Browdie, Kathleen O'Mara, Jordan Jones, and Peter Stine.

And thanks to several friends for their editorial generosity: Marnie Mueller, Henry Flesh, and Deborah Adelman. Also, thanks for help from Fiona Giles, Ron Kolm, Janyce Stefan-Cole, and Gregory Harvey.

Finally, many thanks to Nancy J. Peters and Bob Sharrard at City Lights, and to Ellen Levine and the staff at the Ellen Levine Agency.

These stories have appeared in the following anthologies and magazines, some in slightly different form: "Pandora's Box" in *O. Henry Prize Stories, 1994* (Doubleday) and *Witness;* "Elvis, Axl, and Me" in *Mondo Elvis* (St. Martin's Press); "Jimmy Dean: My Kind of Guy" in *Mondo James Dean* (St. Martin's Press); "The Celibacy Club" in the *Village Voice Literary Supplement;* "Teen Idol" in *Asylum Arts;* "Barbie Goes to Group Therapy" in *Mississippi Valley Review;* "A Spy in the Land of the Ladies Who Lunch" in *Bakunin;* "Ladies with Long Hair" in *Phoebe;* "Health" in *Nobodaddies;* "Cruise Control" in *Buffalo Spree;* "Nautilus" in *Spec;* "The Ping-Pong Vampire" in *Chiron Review;* "The Murder of Juanita Appel" in *13th Moon;* and "Making Love, Making Movies" in *Witness.*

CONTENTS

Elvis, Axl, and Me

I MET ELVIS FOR THE FIRST TIME IN the deli across the street from the elevated line on White Plains Road and Pelham Parkway in the Bronx. Elvis was the only customer besides me. He was sitting at the next table. I could tell it was him right away, even though he was dressed up as a Hasidic Jew. He was wearing a yarmulke on top of his head, and a lopsided, shiny black wig with long peyes on the sides that drooped past his chin, a fake-looking beard to his collarbone, and a shapeless black coat, which didn't hide his paunch, even sitting down. His skin was as white as flour, and his eyes looked glazed, as though he spent far too much time indoors.

"I'll have that soup there, with the round balls floatin' in it," he said to the elderly waiter. He pointed at a large vat of matzoh ball soup. Elvis's Yiddish accent was so bad he might as well have held up a sign saying, "Hey, it's me, Elvis Presley, the Hillbilly Hassid, and I ain't dead at all!" But the waiter, who was wearing a huge hearing aid, just nodded, not appearing to notice anything unusual about his customer.

Sipping my coffee, I stared surreptitiously at Elvis, amazed that he was alive and pretending to be a Hasidic Jew on Pelham Parkway. Unlike all those Elvis-obsessed women who made annual pilgrimages to Graceland and who'd voted on the Elvis postage stamp, I'd never particularly had a thing for Elvis. Elvis just wasn't my type. He was too goody-goody for me. Even back when I was a little girl and I'd watched him swiveling his hips on *The Ed Sullivan Show,* I could tell that, underneath, he was just an All-American Kid.

My type is Axl Rose, the tattooed bad boy lead singer of the heavy metal band Guns n' Roses, whom I'd recently had a *very* minor nervous breakdown over. Although I've never met Axl Rose in the flesh, and although he's *very* immature and *very* politically incorrect, I know that, somehow, somewhere, I *will* meet him one day, because I know that he's destined to be the great love of my life.

Still, even though Elvis is a lot older, tamer, and fatter than Axl, he *is* the King of Rock 'n' Roll, and that's nothing to scoff at. Even Axl himself would have to be impressed by Elvis.

I waited until Elvis's soup had arrived before going over to him. Boldly, I sat right down at his table. "Hey, Elvis," I said, "it's nice to see you."

He looked at me with surprise, nervously twirling one of his fake peyes. And then he blushed, a long, slow blush, and I could tell two things: one, he liked my looks, and two, he wasn't at all sorry that I'd recognized him.

"Why, hon," he said, in his charming, sleepy-sounding voice, "you're the prettiest darn thing I've seen here on Pelham Parkway in a hound dog's age. You're also the first person who's ever really spotted me. All those other Elvis sightings, at Disneyland and shopping malls in New Jersey, you know, they're all bogus as three-dollar bills. I've been right here on Pelham Parkway the whole darned time."

"Tell me *all* about it, Elvis." I leaned forward on my elbows, feeling very flirtatious, the way I used to when I was still living downtown in the East Village. That was before I'd moved back here to Pelham Parkway, where I grew up. The reason I moved back was because, the year before, I inherited my parents' two-bedroom apartment on Holland Avenue, after their tragic death when the chartered bus taking them to Atlantic City had crashed into a Mack truck. During my East Village days, though, I'd had lots of flirtations, as well as lots and lots of dramatic and tortured affairs with angry-looking, spike-haired poets and painters. But all that was before I discovered Axl Rose, of course, and before I had my *very* minor nervous breakdown over him. I mean, my break-down was so minor I didn't do anything crazy at all. I didn't stand in the middle of the street directing traffic, or jump off the Brooklyn Bridge, or anything like that. Mostly I just had a wonderful time fantasizing about what it would be like to make love to him, what it would be like to bite his sexy pierced nipple, to run my fingers through his long, sleek, red hair and all over his many tattoos, and to stick my hand inside his skintight, nearly see-through, white Lycra biking shorts. In the meantime, though, since I had happily bid good-rid-dance to the spike-haired poets and painters, and since Axl Rose wasn't anywhere around, I figured I might as well do some heavy flirting with Elvis.

"Okay," Elvis smiled, almost shyly, "I'll tell you the truth." His teeth were glistening white and perfectly capped, defi-nitely not the teeth of a Hasidic Jew. "And the truth, little girl, is that I'd gotten mighty burned out."

I liked hearing him call me that—"little girl." Mindy, the social worker assigned to my case at the hospital after my breakdown, used to say, "Nancy, you're not a little girl any longer, and rock stars like their women really young. Do you truly believe — I'll be brutal and honest here, it's for your own good—that if, somehow, you actually were to run into Axl Rose on the street, he would even look your way?" Mindy was a big believer in a branch of therapy called "Reality Therapy," which I'd overheard some of the other social workers calling "Pseudo-Reality Therapy" behind her back. Mindy was only twenty-three, and she'd actually had the nerve to laugh in my face when I tried to explain to her that ultimately it would be my womanly, sophisticated, and knowing mind that would make Axl go wild with uncontrollable lust, the kind of lust no vacuous twenty-three-year-old bimbo could ever evoke in a man. Axl and I were destined for each other precisely *because* we were so different, and together we would create a kind of magic sensuality unequaled in the history of the world and, in addition, I would educate him, change him, and help him to grow into a sensitive, mature, and socially concerned male. But Mindy had stopped listening to me. So after that, I changed my strategy. I kept agreeing with her, instead. "You're right, Mindy," I would declare emphatically, "Axl Rose is a spoiled rock 'n' roll superstar and a sexist pig who probably likes jailbait, and there's no way our paths are ever going to cross. I'm not obsessed with him any more. You can sign my release papers now."

"Little girl," Elvis repeated that first day in the deli, maybe sensing how much I liked hearing him say those words, "I ain't gonna go into all the grisly details about myself. You've read the newspapers and seen those soppy TV movies, right?"

I nodded.

"I figured you had," he sighed, stirring his soup. "Everyone has. There ain't been no stone left unturned — even the way I had to wear diapers after a while," he blushed again, "and the way I used my gun to shoot out the TV set, and all that other stuff I did, and how the pressures of being The King, the greatest rock 'n' roll singer in the world, led me to booze, drugs, compulsive overeatin', and impotence. . . ."

I nodded again, charmed by the way he pronounced it im*po*tence with the accent in the middle. My heart went out to him, because he looked so sad and yet so proud of himself at the same time. And I really, really liked that he'd called me *little girl* twice.

"Want some of this here soup?" he offered. "I ain't never had none better."

I shook my head. "Go on, Elvis," I said. "Tell me more." I was really enjoying myself. True, he wasn't Axl, but he *was* The King.

"Well," he said, taking a big bite out of the larger of the two matzoh balls left in his bowl, "what I decided to do, see, was to fake my own death and then spend the rest of my life hiding out, somewhere where nobody would ever think to look, somewhere where I could lead a clean, sober, and pious life." He flirtatiously wiggled his fake peyes at me. "And little girl, that's when I remembered an article I'd read, about how the Bronx is called 'The Forgotten Borough,' because nobody, but *nobody*, with any power or money, ever comes up here."

"I can vouch for that," I agreed, sadly. "I grew up here."

"And, hon, I did it. I cleaned myself up. I ain't a drug and booze addict no more. As for the overeatin', well, even the Good Lord must have one or two vices, is the way I see it." He smiled.

I smiled back, reminding myself that, after all, not everyone can be as wiry and trim as a tattooed rock 'n' roll singer at the height of his career.

"And I ain't im*po*tent no more," Elvis added, leering suggestively at me.

Of course, he had completely won me over. I invited him home with me after he'd finished his soup and the two slices of honey cake he'd ordered for dessert. When we got back to my parents' apartment, he grew hungry again. I went into the kitchen and cooked some kreplach for him. My obese Bubba Sadie had taught me how to make kreplach when I was ten years old, although, before meeting Elvis, I hadn't ever made it on my own.

"Little girl, I just love Jewish food," Elvis told me sincerely, spearing a kreplach with his fork. "I'm so honored that you whipped this up on my humble account."

Elvis ate three servings of my kreplach. He smacked his lips. "Better than my own momma's fried chicken," he said, which I knew was a heapful of praise coming from him, since, according to the newspapers and TV movies, Elvis had an unresolved thing for his mother. It was my turn to blush. And then he stood up and, looking deeply and romantically into my eyes, sang "Love Me Tender." And although his voice showed the signs of age, and the wear and tear of booze and drugs, it was still a beautiful voice, and tears came to my eyes.

After that, we cleared the table, and we went to bed. He wasn't a bad lover, despite his girth. "One thing I do know," he said, again sounding simultaneously humble and proud, "is how to pleasure a woman."

I didn't tell him that night about my obsessive love for Axl Rose, and I'm very glad that I didn't. Because since then I've learned that Elvis has no respect at all for contemporary rock 'n' roll singers. "Pretty boy wussies with hair," he describes them. He always grabs the TV remote away from me and changes the channel when I'm going around the stations and happen to land on MTV. Once, before he was able to change the channel, we caught a quick glimpse together of Axl, strutting in front of the mike in his sexy black leather kilt and singing his pretty heart out about some cruel woman who'd hurt him and who he intended to hurt back. I held my breath, hoping that Elvis, sitting next to me on my mother's pink brocade sofa, wouldn't hear how rapidly my heart was beating, wouldn't see that my skin was turning almost as pink as the sofa.

"What a momma's boy and wussey *that* skinny li'l wanna-be rock 'n' roller is," Elvis merely sneered, exaggerating his own drawl and grabbing the remote out of my hand. He switched to HBO, which was showing an old Burt Reynolds movie. "Hot dawg," Elvis said, settling back on the sofa, "a Burt flick!"

Still, sometimes when we're in bed, I make a mistake and call him Axl. And he blinks and looks at me and says, "Huh? What'd you say, little girl?" "Oh, Elvis, darling," I always answer without missing a beat, "I just said "Ask." Ask me to do anything for you, anything at all, and I'll do it. Just ask." And really, I've grown so fond of him, and we have such fun together, that I mean it. I *would* do anything for Elvis. It isn't his fault that Axl Rose, who captured my heart first, is my destiny.

Elvis and I lead a simple, sweet life together. He comes over three or four times every week in his disguise — the yarmulke, the fake beard and peyes, the shapeless black coat — and we take little strolls together through Bronx Park. Then, when he grows tired, we head back to my parents' apartment, and I cook dinner for him. In addition to my kreplach, he's crazy about my blintzes and noodle kugel.

After dinner, we go to bed, where he pleasures me, and I fantasize about Axl. Later, we put our clothes back on, and we sit side by side on my mother's sofa and watch Burt Reynolds movies. Sometimes we watch Elvis's old movies, too. His favorites are *Jailhouse Rock* and *Viva Las Vegas*. But they always make him weepy and sad, which breaks my heart, so I prefer to watch Burt Reynolds.

And Elvis is content just to keep on dating. He never pressures me to move in with him, or to get married, which — as much as I care for him — is fine with me. "Little girl," Elvis always says, "I love you with all my country boy's heart and soul, more than I ever loved Priscilla, I swear I do, and there ain't a selfish bone in my body, but my rent-controlled apartment on a tree-lined block, well, it's a once-in-a-lifetime deal, so I just can't give it up and move into your parents' apartment with you."

"Hey, Elvis, no sweat," I reply, sweetly. And I tell him that, much as I love him, I can't move in with him, either, because *his* apartment — a studio with kitchenette — is just too small for both of us. "I understand, little girl," he says, hugging me. "I really do. You've got some of that feisty women's libber inside of you, and you need your own space."

But the truth is, it's not my space I care about so much. The truth is that I've got long-range plans, which don't include Elvis. Here's how I figure it: down the road, when Axl, like Elvis before him, burns out — and it's inevitable that he will, given the way that boy is going — when he's finally driven, like Elvis, to fake his own death in order to escape the pressures of rock 'n' roll superstardom, and when he goes into hiding under an assumed identity, well, then, I think the odds are pretty good he'll end up living right here on Pelham Parkway. After all, Axl and I are *bound* to meet up some day — destiny is destiny, and there's no way around it.

I'm not saying it *will* happen just that way, mind you. All I'm saying is that, if Elvis Presley is alive and well and masquerading as a Hasidic Jew in the Bronx, well, then, anything is possible, and I do mean *anything*. And anything includes me and Axl, right here on Pelham Parkway, pleasuring each other night and day. It's not that I want to hurt Elvis, believe me. But I figure he probably won't last long enough to see it happen, anyway, considering how out of shape he is, and all.

The way I picture it is this: Axl holding me in his tattooed, wiry arms and telling me that all his life he's been waiting to find me, even though he hardly dared dream that I existed in the flesh, the perfect woman, an experienced woman who can make kreplach and blintzes and noodle kugel, a woman who was the last—and best—lover of Elvis Presley, the King of Rock 'n' Roll himself. It *could* happen. That's all I'm saying.

★ ★ ★

The Celibacy Club

Why I Joined the Celibacy Club

I WAS CURLED UP ON MY BED IN MY pink cotton nightgown. It was a rainy Saturday night. Ichabod, my cat, was curled up beside me. I was in the process of devouring an entire pint of chocolate/marsh-mallow/walnut/raisin ice cream, trying to fight off the hic-cups, and watching a late-night cable TV show on the porn channel, all at the same time. I don't know why I chose to watch the porn channel that night. I'd never watched it before. I'd never even watched a cable station before.

I suppose my watching it had something to do with the fact that I was depressed. The month before, I'd been laid off from my job on Wall Street. And, in addition to the blow to my ego, I was flat broke. I'd been the kind of Wall Street "gal," as we were called, who kept her hair immaculately *coiffed*—colored, styled, and permed—and who wore expensive, crisp linen jackets with football player–size shoulder pads, and sexy but businesslike slim skirts that always ended a discreet inch above the knee. But that night, I'd taken a long, hard look at my bankbook, and it had become obvious to me that I wasn't going to be buying any more linen jackets and slim skirts for a while. So maybe that was why I was home alone, on a rainy Saturday night, watching a porn show with nobody but Ichabod to keep me company.

The star of the porn show was a stripper. A skinny, hyperactive woman with long, straight hair riddled with split ends. She was prancing around in a barely-there, crocheted bikini, and she had two guests with her. The two guests were also prancing around. One was a man with frizzy yellow hair, a potbelly, and spindly legs. He was naked except for a leopard-skin bathing suit, which looked as though he'd stuffed the front of it with a large chicken drumstick.

The stripper's other guest was a black woman with a shaved head, a tattoo on her forehead of what might have been either a leopard or a fist, I couldn't be sure, and a ring through her nose. She was completely naked, and her breasts looked like two bowling balls, hard and unyielding. The stripper and her two guests were singing a song together as they pranced around. They slurred the words, and none of them could carry a tune, and they kept licking their lips and lewdly rolling their eyes while they sang.

I didn't know whether to laugh or cry. "Ichabod," I said mournfully, digging my spoon deeper into the container of ice cream, and still hiccuping away, "look at those people. Will you just *look* at them?"

Ichabod looked at the three prancing figures on the screen. Then he turned his bright yellow eyes back on me.

"People actually find this kind of pathetic stuff sexy," I explained to him. Since I had the hiccups, I had to speak slowly and take deep breaths between each word. "It's unbelievable, I know, Ichabod, but this," I said, shaking my head, "passes for sexual entertainment!"

Ichabod blinked.

"I agree with you entirely, Ichabod," I said. "It *is* horrible. And, I, for one, don't ever want to have sex again! Ever, ever, ever. I swear to you, I'd rather be celibate!" My own passion surprised me. It occurred to me that I'd just spoken the absolute truth. I *would* rather be celibate. In fact, from that moment on, I decided, I would be! No more late-night clubs. No more blind dates. No more summer shares in beach houses. I said the word aloud: "celibate." The soft *c*. The hard *b*. It sounded like "masturbate." Or "jailbait." "Ichabod," I said, licking the last bit of ice cream off my spoon, "It may not have been my choice to be laid off, but it's my choice never to be laid!" Ichabod blinked thoughtfully, and then he began coughing up a hairball.

How I Found the Celibacy Club

It was just an unassuming ad in the back of one of those free neighborhood newspapers. The *Midtown Maverick*, I think it's called. Or maybe the *Midtown Maven*. It was smack in the middle of a page filled with ads for fitness trainers who could make you look exactly like Arnold Schwarzenegger in a mere two weeks. There were also ads for psychic channelers who would put you in touch with Freud, Marx, and J. D. Rockefeller for a mere five hundred dollars. And, naturally, there were ads for phone sex — call "1-800-NIPPLE!" — and for escort services promising you an evening with "young Oriental girls devoted to your every need!"

The ad for the Celibacy Club was much smaller than those others. All it said was, CELIBACY CLUB SEEKS NEW MEMBERS, WEEKLY MEETINGS. UPTOWN LOCATION. And it gave a phone number. So I called. A machine answered, and a woman's recorded voice came on. "The Celibacy Club meets once a month," she said, huskily. The way she said the word — celibacy — made me hear it a whole new way, as in *celebrate*. "We meet in the Bronx," she went on. "New members, of all genders, colors, classes, and religious persuasions are welcome." And then she recited a number to call for further information. Still, although I was intrigued at the prospect of meeting like-minded, celibate souls, I really didn't have any desire to shlep all the way up to the Bronx. Besides, I'd heard that the Bronx could be very dangerous.

But I went ahead and called the second number, anyway. This time the recorded voice was a man's. He sounded very full of himself and overly sincere, like some kind of would-be charismatic religious leader. He gave the date and time of the next meeting, and then he gave traveling information. He was very thorough: He gave information on how to get there by car, express bus, or subway. When I'd finished writing down all of his directions, Ichabod jumped into my lap. I stroked his grey fur. "Pray for me, Ichabod," I said. "I'm going to the Bronx." I repeated it — "the Bronx." It sounded like "bronze," which reminded me of the sexy skin of the lifeguards at the midtown health club where I swam every morning, although it was looking as though I wasn't going to be able to keep up my membership payments much longer.

The First Meeting of the Celibacy Club

I wore a modest grey suit and a white man-tailored shirt, and I decided to take the express bus. I couldn't afford a taxi, and the express bus sounded a lot safer than the subway. The midtown bus stop was on Madison Avenue, in front of a florist shop with grinning plastic elves in the window. It was five o'clock, rush hour, and about twenty people were already lined up at the bus stop when I got there. The bus was packed when it arrived, and so all twenty of us had to stand. While the bus made its slow, bumpy way up Madison, through Harlem, and into the Bronx, it occurred to me that maybe I wasn't the only person riding uptown to the Celibacy Club. The woman standing next to me, whose elbow kept poking me in the ribs, was reading a romance novel, one of those bodice-rippers they sell on supermarket checkout lines, and the man next to her had a Walkman on, with salsa music blasting from it. They both struck me as possible candidates.

But when the bus came to my stop, I got off alone. The bus stop was right in front of the entrance to the Bronx Zoo, an institution I'd always meant to pay a visit to, but working on Wall Street and all, I'd never had much time. I was tempted to go in right then, for a quick peek at the penguins and the gorillas, if nothing else, but I didn't want to be late for my first meeting of the Celibacy Club, so I resisted.

I walked a block or so past the zoo entrance, and I found myself in a neighborhood called Pelham Parkway. One of the first things I saw was a porn theater, which was showing a film called *Sorority Sluts from Hell*. I walked along White Plains Road, beneath the elevated subway tracks, and I stared at the people around me, the people of the Bronx. Pelham Parkway seemed to be a regular melting pot, with every ethnic group imaginable. There were lots of children sucking lollypops, and lots of mothers. The mothers from every ethnic group were wearing polyester pantsuits with explosive, colorful patterns. I passed a noisy Off-Track Betting

Center, and a few Greek coffee shops. There were also lots of electronics stores advertising discount prices on Walkmen, stereos, and CD players. And there were an inordinate amount, it seemed to me, of shoe stores. Shoes for all size feet, especially for difficult-to-fit feet. I made a mental note of that, since I wear a Triple-A width. Not that I'm complaining. I don't really mind having very narrow feet. In fact, I think that narrow feet are sexier than wide feet. The only thing I mind, and I particularly minded it right then, having just been laid off, is how difficult and expensive it is to find shoes that fit. So I was tempted to try on an inexpensive but very sexy pair of super-narrow patent-leather high heels that I saw in the window of a shoestore called Betty Lee. But I resisted that, too.

The directions I'd written down led me to a large brick building on a pretty, tree-lined street called Holland Avenue. There was a sign outside the building advertising co-ops for sale. I wondered who in their right mind would buy a co-op in the Bronx. I mean, what could the resale value possibly be? On the other hand, I had to acknowledge that I was no longer one to talk. My own fancy midtown building was going co-op, sure, but because I was now broke and unemployed, I wasn't even going to be able to buy my studio at the insider's price.

A young Hispanic woman and a little boy were sitting on the stoop. The woman was pretty, with long, dyed red hair done up with glittery bows, like a country and western singer's. But the child was one of the ugliest little boys I'd ever seen in my life. He was about eight, and he was pimply, shifty-eyed, and surly-looking. "Get up, *hijo*," his mother said to him, "and make some room for the lady to pass." He gave me a long, dirty look before obeying her. "Mama," I heard him say as I headed toward the elevator, "I bet that lady is going up to the fifth floor, to the club for losers!"

I rang the bell for apartment 5-C. C for celibacy, I guessed. The door was opened by a large black woman. Her greying hair was pulled tightly into a severe bun on top of her head, and she was wearing a dignified herringbone suit. "First time?" she asked me, before I'd even stepped inside. Her voice was loud and vibrant, very much alive, in contrast to the severity of her suit and her hairstyle.

I nodded. "Yes. First time."

"Well, feast your eyes," she said, holding up her left hand.

I wasn't sure what I was supposed to be looking at. "Very attractive nail polish," I said, hesitantly.

"No," she said. "Not the polish. The ring!" She wriggled her hand at me. "I'm married *and* celibate," she winked. "That's me. So don't think for a minute that this club is a lonely hearts, singles-only club. No way. Curtis, my husband, is inside with the group. He's married and celibate, too. He'd damn well *better* be," she said, winking at me again. "No, seriously, honey, this is a club for informed people who make choices. Not for losers, or misfits, or sexually frustrated anal-compulsive types. Not at all."

"Good," I said, trying to smile. "I'm glad to hear it."

"I'm Cora," she said, leading me into a living room, which was filled with large potted plants and paintings of brown-skinned island girls with flowers in their hair and naked breasts the sizes of melons. About six or seven people were sitting in a circle on brown canvas director's chairs. On a shellacked, tree-trunk coffee table in the center of the room sat a glass bowl filled with potato chips.

A man of about sixty rose to greet me. He had a gold hoop earring in one ear, and a shock of white hair that went to his shoulders. He was wearing a white T-shirt, snug-fitting blue jeans, and bright yellow rubber thongs on his feet. His toenails needed to be cut. He held out his hand to me. "I'm Bob," he said. I recognized his voice as the charismatic one on the answering machine. "And this is my apartment," he gestured around the room, "but I am most definitely *not* the leader."

"We have no leader," Cora said.

"Sit down," Bob told me.

I sat down in one of the brown director's chairs.

"It's true, we have no leader here, and no followers, either," a woman sitting directly across from me said. Her voice sounded like the husky female voice I'd heard on the answering machine. She had long blond hair with split ends and a big white smile, and she reminded me of the stripper on the cable-TV porn show.

"So tell us about yourself," Bob urged me. Smiling, he folded his hands in his lap.

All of the other group members looked expectantly at me. The woman who looked like the stripper munched loudly on a potato chip.

"My name is Nancy," I said. "I live in midtown Manhattan." I couldn't think of anything else to say.

The group members murmured enthusiastically among themselves, as though this was extremely interesting information.

"I live in midtown, too," a handsome man on my left said. He had an Italian accent. "I live right near Trump Tower. I hope that we are neighbors." His skin was tan, and his eyes were a rich brown color. He was wearing a cream-colored, fitted linen suit, and he had matching, creamy leather loafers on his feet. In any other group, I would have been sure he was flirting with me. But his rich brown eyes were devoid of sexual comment. "Do you own or rent your apartment?" he went on.

"I rent," I said softly, wishing more than ever that I hadn't been laid off.

"Ah," he said, cooly and asexually, "I own mine, you see."

Cora interrupted. "Now, Nancy," she said eagerly, "in any other group, even, let's say, a namby-pamby group like Overeater's Anonymous, you would think that Giorgio was trying to put the moves on you, wouldn't you?"

I nodded, feeling sheepish, wondering how Cora had been able to read my mind. I didn't look at Giorgio.

"But not here," Cora went on. "Not Giorgio. Not in the Celibacy Club."

"Nancy," Giorgio said, in his Italian accent, "I've been celibate for three years, you see. And I never miss a meeting of the club. So," he laughed, showing teeth so white and perfect they were undoubtedly capped, "you have nothing to fear from me."

"Come on, Nancy," Bob smiled at me again, sounding more charismatic than ever, "tell us some more about yourself."

"I used to work on Wall Street, but I was laid off," I admitted. "Hard times, you know. Nothing personal. At least that's what they said." There were more sympathetic murmurs. "I live alone. I have a cat. Ichabod." "Nancy," Bob asked, leaning forward, looking extremely concerned. "How did you come to your celibacy?"

I shrugged. I tried to meet Bob's eyes while I spoke. "I'm not really sure. It's all pretty recent. Just since I was laid off. Before that, I had plenty of boyfriends. Guys down on Wall Street. We did the club scene. We knew how to have fun and be safe, too. I was on the pill. My breasts ached. I'm glad to be off that, I can tell you. But other than my aching breasts, I was happy. At least, I thought I was. But then, when I was laid off, I thought, hey, sex with these guys is so bland, really. I'd just never noticed it before. It was a big nothing. A zero. It had no . . . taste."

"Tasteless," Cora echoed, nodding happily and waving her wedding ring finger at me. "That's right, honey. That's exactly what Curtis and I decided. In and out, wham and bam and all that. It's got no flavor, no sauce, no spice, no tang. Sex, today, in the US of A, for married and unmarried alike, is tasteless!"

"Amen," a black man with a pointed beard who was sitting next to Cora said. I figured that he was Curtis. "Tasteless," he went on, "like chicken soup." He and Cora started to laugh.

And then everyone laughed. And then, Bob, who I was having a difficult time not thinking of as the group leader, asked us all to repeat Cora's words—"Sex is like chicken soup!" So everyone repeated it. And then they kept repeating it. I joined in on the third repetition, and, like everyone else, I got louder and louder as I repeated it. I also helped myself to a few potato chips. I smiled at the woman who looked like the stripper on cable TV. She smiled back. I winked at Cora and Curtis. I even managed to meet Giorgio's asexual, deep-set Italian eyes.

Bob rose from his director's chair and went into the kitchen. When he returned he was carrying a large, creamy-looking chocolate cake. We all cut ourselves big slices.

"Now, *this,* unlike sex," Cora said, taking a bite, "has flavor!" Curtis nodded. Giorgio smiled asexually at me and licked some creamy icing off his fingers.

The Second Meeting of the Celibacy Club

I felt braver, much less afraid of the Bronx and Pelham Parkway. So I rode uptown on the subway. It was four-thirty, not quite rush hour, and the only other people in my car were one homeless man and three teenage girls. We'd all gotten on together at 72nd Street. I sat down in the far right corner, the homeless man fell asleep immediately in the far left corner, and the girls sat together in the center of the car, listening to a large radio they set up on the floor in front of them. The radio was tuned to a station that seemed to play only Whitney Houston songs. The girls snapped their fingers and sang along. Their voices weren't bad, although they couldn't hit Whitney's high notes.

In the South Bronx, around Simpson Street, one of the girls got up from her seat and came over to me. She stood above me, and I looked up at her. She had blond hair with black roots, cut short and spiky, and she wore bright pink stretch pants and a white tank top. "Lady," she said, "you got a cigarette?"

"Sorry, I don't smoke," I said, truthfully. "I gave it up."

"That's okay," she said, nodding. Her two friends, who'd shut off their radio, came over and joined us. The three of them stood over me, swaying as the car moved.

"So, lady, maybe you got some condoms you can lend us, instead?" The one who asked me this was wearing a red Lycra minidress. "We're too broke to buy them, and we wanna have safe sex. Help us out. Give us a break, okay?"

"Sorry," I repeated, again truthfully. "I don't carry condoms. I gave up sex, too." But I reached inside my wallet, and, even though I was broke, I gave them each a few dollars for condoms.

Then the girls sat down next to me. They turned the radio back on, and this time I sang along with them to Whitney Houston's songs. When the subway rolled into the Pelham Parkway stop, I stood up. "Bye-bye, girls," I said.

The third girl walked me to the subway doors. She wore mirrored sunglasses and a red leather headband around her forehead. "Hey, lady," she said, as I stepped out of the car, "why'd you give up sex?"

I shrugged. "It's bland, like chicken soup." I stood on the subway platform and faced her.

She took off her mirrored sunglasses and rolled her eyes at me. "No it ain't, lady," she said, "at least, not with my boyfriend it ain't!"

The subway doors closed.

This time, as I walked along White Plains Road, I spotted a pair of subtle white leather pumps in the window of Betty Lee's. I went inside and held them in my hand. The leather felt tempting, soft, and glovelike. But I resisted. I placed them back down, nodding farewell to the shoestore clerk, who was eyeing me hopefully, and I headed over to Holland Avenue.

The pretty Hispanic woman was sitting on the stoop again. She had even more glittering bows in her hair, and this time, she had two boys with her. That ugly little boy actually had a twin brother! The sight of the two of them sitting there, with snot dripping from their noses, was enough to turn anyone celibate forever, I thought. "Make way for the lady," the mother admonished both of the boys this time. Although they gave me filthy looks, they did rise so that I could step inside. "Mama, that's the loser lady again," I heard one of them whine, as I pressed the elevator button.

The elevator creaked its way up to the fifth floor. Cora answered the door again. She winked at me and led me into the living room. I noticed immediately that the group was larger by two — a new female member and a new male member.

"This is Nancy's second meeting," Cora announced to the two new members, as I sat down in one of the brown director's chairs.

Feeling proud, like an old pro, I smiled at the two new-comers, and I helped myself to a potato chip.

Bob urged the two new members to speak.

"My name is Madga," the new female member said. She was wearing a low-cut blouse and a navy blue leather skirt. She spoke with some sort of an Eastern European accent. "I'm a sexy, sexy girl, I think."

I tensed, waiting for the men to take advantage of her, to make lewd remarks at her expense. But of course, that was foolish of me, because this was the Celibacy Club, not a mud-wrestling club, and so none of them did. Instead, they all murmured sympathetically. I peeked at Giorgio. This time, the color of his linen suit and matching loafers was a pale peach. He was staring at Madga in his special, asexual way.

"Go on, Madga," Bob urged, sincerely and charismatically.

"Men lust after me," Madga said, crossing her plump legs. "And I've gotten used to spreading my legs to get what I want," she uncrossed her legs and spread them to illustrate her point. The men clucked sympathetically again. Giorgio averted his deep, asexual eyes, as though in sorrow at the spectacle. "But I don't want to keep spreading my legs for the rest of my life, even though I've gotten so good at it." She recrossed her legs. "I want to stop and smell the flowers instead. Because," she went on triumphantly, "today is the first day of the rest of my life!"

"Madga," Bob said, "we'll get back to you soon." He turned to the new male member.

"I'm Paul," the new man said. He was skinny and bald and bearded. He seemed shy and nervous. "I'm afraid I just don't understand the whole concept of safe sex."

"Oh," Madga laughed, "it's no big deal, just use a rubber."

"That's not what I mean," Paul said, sadly.

"Go on, Paul, we're listening," Bob urged, sincerely.

"What I mean is this. I'm a timid man. And, for me, sex meant risk. The only risk I was ever willing to take in my entire life. I'm an accountant. I'm afraid of heights and deep water and airplanes. But I had no sexual fears. None. I was a wild man in the bedroom, in the bars. I *was!*" He sounded defiant, as though daring us not to believe him.

"I believe you, man," Curtis said. "Don't worry."

"Me, too," Cora said.

"We all believe you, Paul," Bob said, comfortingly. "Go on."

"But now they say that sex can be more than just risky. Now they say it can cause death. And I don't want to die. Now they say you can't have wild sex with strangers any more. Find out everything you can about your partner months in advance, they say. Spend months getting to know each other platonically. Then watch safe-sex videos at night and snuggle up and sip hot chocolate together. Well, I'm sorry, but I'm just not happy about that. It was the risk, the unknown, that thrilled me. Without it, who cares? I might as well just stay home and watch that skinny, tacky-looking stripper and her weird-looking guests on cable TV."

I looked across the circle at the woman who looked like the tacky-looking stripper on cable TV. She was staring at Paul and munching loudly on a potato chip.

"Paul, do you know what I think?" Cora asked loudly.

"What?" He stared glumly at his kneecaps.

"What I think is that sex is like chicken soup!'

"Yes," Madga agreed, spreading her legs again. "Or like spoiled milk that stinks to high heaven!"

Bob urged us all to repeat Madga's line, "Sex is like spoiled milk that stinks to high heaven!" over and over again. We all repeated it. I was enjoying myself again. I snuck a look at Paul. He was repeating it and laughing, too. He didn't look so glum, anymore.

Bob rose and went into the kitchen and returned with an oozing banana cream pie. We all cut ourselves thick slices.

Madga devoured her piece quickly. Cora and Curtis ate their slices slowly this time, staring dreamily into each other's eyes. Asexually, Giorgio cut me a second slice and handed it to me.

The Third Meeting of the Celibacy Club

By the third meeting, I didn't have to choose between the express bus or the subway any longer. Since Giorgio lived nearby, he offered to give me a ride. When he picked me up at my apartment — which I'd spent the whole day cleaning and straightening — he was wearing a beige-colored linen suit and loafers.

He drove a white Mercedes, and I asked him how he dared to park it on the dangerous streets of the Bronx. "Just as I have no sexual desires," he explained, "I have no fears." He was a good driver, assertive but cautious, and he played Rachmaninoff on a cassette player while he drove. I opened the car window on my side, and, leaning my head back against the cushy seat, I allowed the wind to play with my hair, which I'd decided to grow out, since I could no longer afford to have it cut and styled every three weeks. Giorgio, who was driving with one hand on the wheel and the other across the back of the seat, turned to look at me at a red light. "Your hair looks very nice," he said asexually.

A few new members showed up that night. One, a sociologist in a tweed jacket, described sex as a "zero sum game," and we all repeated it at Bob's urging and laughed and ate butterscotch pie.

The Fourth Meeting of the Celibacy Club

Giorgio arrived at my apartment wearing a bronze-colored suit and loafers. My hair had grown to my chin. "How nice you look, Nancy," he said to me, "like that actress in that movie, *Something Wild,* the one who ties up the leading actor with ropes and performs acts of sexual bondage with him."

At that meeting, Michael, a dancer who was wearing a flowing, floor-length Moroccan caftan, said that "sex is like a pulled muscle," and we all repeated it and laughed and ate mocha cream pie.

The Fifth Meeting of the Celibacy Club

Giorgio was wearing an ivory-colored suit and loafers. He said that my hair, which had, by then, completely lost its perm, looked "lovely, just like a vulnerable, needy, pouty-mouthed British fashion model's from the 1960s."

At that meeting, Juliette, a legal secretary who was wearing a grey jumpsuit and sneakers, wept and said that sex was painful for her, and that she found nudity ugly, and Bob urged us to hug her and to tell her that we all cared about her. And we all hugged her asexually and then we ate chocolate chip cookies. Giorgio took a few cookies along with him for our car ride back. We stopped off at O'Neil's and had some martinis — he drank his shaken, not stirred, just like James Bond — and then we sat on a stone bench in Damrosch Park and listened to the marching band that was playing in the bandshell.

Why I Dropped Out of the Celibacy Club

The night of the sixth meeting, Giorgio arrived at my apartment ten minutes early. He was wearing tight black jeans, black boots, a black leather jacket, and black sunglasses with steel frames. "I drove my bike," he said, standing in the living room with one hand on his hip, and placing his booted foot on the top of my glass coffee table, "instead of my Mercedes."

My hair was so long by then that I'd pulled it off my neck into a ponytail and tied it with a scarlet ribbon that matched the scarlet-colored silk dress I was wearing.

And, I don't know exactly how it happened — who did what to whom first — but we began to kiss. Passionately and repeatedly. And then we fell together onto the sofa, and then we ended up naked on the living room rug. We never even made it into my bedroom. And after we had sex once, we had sex again. And while we had sex, we said, in rhythm, "It's not like chicken soup or spoiled milk or a pulled muscle, and it's not painful and ugly, either." And we had sex all night long, in what seemed like millions and trillions of positions. I was having a wonderful time — it felt so good after all those months of celibacy — and I was secretly hoping to burn off some of those damned pounds I'd put on from all of Bob's cakes and pies and cookies.

Giorgio and I never did make it to the meeting that night. He spent the night in my apartment. We had breakfast the next morning at O'Neil's. "Our special place," he said, but we both knew he was being gently ironic, and that we weren't going to see each other again. Which was okay by me. I liked him fine, of course, but I didn't *love* him. He and I had experienced some of that age-old, mysterious chemistry, that was all. But, I realized, that was more — much more — than enough.

And I never did see Cora or Curtis or Bob or Madga or Paul or the woman who looked like the tacky stripper on cable TV or any of the rest of them, either, after that night. And I didn't miss them. To my surprise, what I did miss was Pelham Parkway. Such a nice, thriving, unpretentious neighborhood. An ideal neighborhood for someone who was unemployed and who had gotten sick and tired of demeaning job interviews during which she was forced to sit and listen to baby-faced, coke-addicted guys in pinstriped suits tell her why they couldn't afford to hire her unless she was willing to start back down at the bottom of the career ladder, typing and filing and answering phones.

So one day, on a whim, to give myself a little treat during those hard times, I rode the subway up to Pelham Parkway, and I headed right for Betty Lee's, and I bought the high-heeled patent-leather shoes. And then I went back a few weeks after that, and I bought the soft white leather pumps. And then, eventually, I found a new job. It wasn't glamorous. It wasn't on a fast track. It was a public relations position in the Community Affairs Department at Bronx Municipal Hospital Center, which was located right there, on Pelham Parkway. And, after about a year or so, I saved up enough money for a small down payment, and then I bought myself a nice little co-op apartment about five minutes from the hospital, on one of those pretty, tree-lined little streets.

It took Ichabod a couple of weeks to adjust to the new location of his litter box. But since then I honestly can say that he and I have never been happier. I have two boyfriends now. One's a doctor at the hospital, and one works at a construction site nearby. I love to go to the zoo on weekends, sometimes alone, and sometimes with my boyfriends, both of whom have soft spots for animals. And I've grown especially fond of the exotic birds.

I also canceled my subscription to cable TV, since I get good reception up here. So I never saw the porn show again, which is just as well, really. Although now and then, I do think I see the tacky-looking, skinny stripper — the *real* stripper, not the woman in the Celibacy Club who looked so much like her—buying shoes in Betty Lee's. I'm probably mistaken, though.

★ ★ ★

Pandora's Box

PANDORA WAS A PHONE SEX WORKER. She worked in an office in a dingy building in SoHo. About six other women worked the shift with her, from eight at night until three in the morning. "I give phone," was the way that some of the other women described what they did. Pandora preferred saying, "I'm a worker in the phone sex industry."

Pandora was not a prostitute. She resented the term "phone whore." Her clients didn't know her real name. They couldn't touch her, see her, give her diseases, make her pregnant. She sold words and images and voices, not her body. Never her body.

Unlike some of the other women with whom she worked, Pandora lived quietly; she didn't drink or take drugs. She didn't trust herself to. She feared that if she allowed herself even one glass of wine, one pill, it would all be over for her. She would be opening a box that wasn't meant to be opened.

Pandora's job didn't pay much. She lived in a dark studio apartment on the first floor of a building on Eighth Avenue, in Times Square, next door to a strip-show joint. The neighborhood was rampant with muggers and crack dealers, but Pandora couldn't afford to move. She kept her hair short and wore loose-fitting jeans and T-shirts, so as not to call attention to herself. And it wasn't as though rich women on Sutton Place never got raped or murdered. Where you lived didn't matter, not really. The world was a dangerous place.

Many of Pandora's clients wanted her to be a dominatrix. As a dominatrix, she used the name Queen Bee. Her slaves liked her to order them to get down on their knees so she could whip them until they bled. They liked for her to humiliate them in various ways — to call them filthy names and pretend she was smearing excrement on them, for instance, and then not allow them to clean themselves up. The slave-men also liked to be ordered to wear diapers. They liked her to shove high-heeled shoes down their throats.

Other of her clients asked Pandora to be a little girl, a little girl who deserved a spanking for being so naughty. She spoke to those clients in a lisping, breathy, singsong voice. She would say, "Oh, Daddy, I've been such a bad, bad little girl!" Those clients knew her by the name of Angela, a name she chose because it sounded angelic and innocent, and because innocence was precisely what those clients wished to abuse.

Sometimes, she was asked to have sex with a dog — usually a mean-looking German shepherd — or a horse.

Frequently, she was raped. She was asked to throw grapefruits at men and to lick the juice off their bodies. She was bound and gagged and tied up with nylon stockings. She was suspended from the ceiling on meat hooks.

She never actually did any of these things. Never. She, herself, was inviolate. Untouchable. Always in control. It was just fantasy, just impersonal dialogue transmitted over phone wires between strangers. The name of the company she worked for was Phantasy Phone-Phun. Pandora never felt sexy, or sensual, over the phone. She believed that what she did was a kind of social work—helping frustrated and lonely men to obtain a small bit of pleasure in their lives. She was also contributing to society, helping to prevent these men from acting out their very dangerous fantasies, from really going out on the street and raping or murdering women. She was offering these men an outlet. She understood their loneliness, their fantasies. In her heart, she knew these men, had always known them.

A lot of the other women at Phantasy Phone-Phun wanted to be glamorous movie stars. Like Pandora, they had fled to New York from small towns and unhappy homes. Most, like Pandora, had never finished high school. But unlike Pandora, the ones who wanted to be movie stars perceived what they did at Phantasy Phone-Phun as theater, as a rehearsal for bigger and better roles to come. Pandora felt sorry for those women because they were deluding themselves. A few of them made porn films, and were hoping to be discovered that way. A few stripped in the strip joint next door to her building in Times Square.

"Pandora, Pandora, come here, Pandora!" her father, the judge, the powerful judge, in the sleepy upstate New York college town, used to call out to her when she was a little girl. She had no choice but to go to him. He would lock the door. "My little girl," he would say, "my little Pandora and her little box." When Pandora got into the big, creaky bed with him, everything turned abruptly to a dream. It had to be a dream, because her real daddy, the man who bought her sweet candies and salty, crunchy pretzel sticks, the man who loved her more than anyone else in the whole world, the man who was respected by all the people in their town — that man would never do anything mean to her. Real daddies didn't hurt their daughters; real daddies protected their daughters. So, she wasn't there, not really, when this dream thing happened with this man who was not her daddy—this man who had stepped right out of her dark nightmares, out of her most frightening and horrid fantasies. Afterward she didn't remember what had happened. She didn't even remember having dreamed him.

When Pandora was a little girl, she resented her name. She'd read the tale of Pandora in a book of mythology for children. She hadn't liked the girl Pandora in the myth, even if she was beautiful and even if her name meant "the gift of all." It seemed to her that the other Pandora was a very, very bad and guilty little girl for doing such a thing, for having so little self-control, for opening the lid of that box and unleashing sorrow and evil and plagues upon the world, despite having been warned never, never to open the box. That other Pandora had too many desires, too much passion, for a nice little girl. And Pandora didn't like the ending of the myth, either, when the other Pandora finds Hope at the bottom of the box, in the guise of a butterfly. The other Pandora must have been a ninny to believe in Hope. Pandora, herself, already knew better than to believe in anything.

One afternoon, her heart racing, she found the courage to tell her father how much she hated her name. In a soft voice, she asked him, please, to change her name to something very simple, like Margaret or Mary. Her father was sitting in the deep brown leather armchair in his wood-paneled den. He poured himself a drink. When she was finished explaining her reasons for hating her name, he spoke very slowly. He said that she should remember that she wasn't the real Pandora from the myth. Nobody blamed her for evil; and at the same time, nobody was forcing her to feel hopeful if she didn't feel that way. Myths aren't real, he said, myths explain the unexplainable, offer rationales for the irrational. He described myths from other cultures: the myth of Gilgamesh from ancient Sumeria; the myth of the Native American trickster. Many people, he told her, believe that the Bible is one big myth. Besides, he said, the world was filled with self-involved, narcissistic people who cared only about themselves, and nobody else really gave a damn whether Pandora was named Pandora or Athena or Aphrodite. He waved his drink and spilled some on his lap, and said he was tired of explaining all this to her. "You're just paranoid, Pandora," he said finally, "and paranoia is the ultimate narcissism."

Paranoia was a major subject in their household, which consisted of Pandora, her two older brothers, and her father. This was because her mother had been diagnosed as a paranoid schizophrenic and was in the hospital. Or, as Pandora liked to say — "in hospital" — the way she'd heard it said by British characters on TV.

Pandora had few memories of her mother, who had died in hospital. These were the memories she did have: herself, as a very little girl in a pink flared dress, watching from her seat on the curb where her mother has deposited her, while her mother stands in the street directing traffic in her ripped ankle-length housedress, until the police come and take her away, and her mother claws and spits at them, as Pandora begins to cry.

Another memory: her mother walking naked in their garden, with a checkered bandanna tied rakishly around her neck, dancing and twirling her arms, shouting, "I am a butterfly!" over and over again, scaring Pandora, who is watching from a window, wondering why her mother is stealing the butterfly image from her myth, wondering if her own sad mother is trying to communicate something to the world about Hope.

And another: her mother not getting out of bed for months and months, so that Pandora has to get ready all by herself for school, has to remember to put her clothes out the night before, has to learn how to iron and wash clothes, how to cook meals for her father and brothers, how to give her father massages just the way he likes them late at night after he's worked all day at the courthouse where he's a very important man, and it's crucial that Pandora learn to relax him just the way he likes, although she hates to do it, hates the way her father's flesh feels beneath her small hands.

When Pandora was in seventh grade, her father wouldn't allow her to go to boy-girl parties even though the parents of all the other girls let their daughters go, as long as the parties were supervised. Her father said that Pandora was not as responsible as the other girls, and that she would get in trouble at an earlier age than the rest of them because she was so vulnerable and silly, because her head was too easily turned by flattery.

On a Saturday afternoon, when she was in ninth grade, she put on a pink, gauzy, short dress that she'd bought at the mall with her allowance money the week before. The dress was so beautiful, she felt like a princess in it. As she stood staring at herself in the mirror, her father walked into her bedroom. He yelled at her and told her to change her clothes, told her that she looked like a tramp. She protested, "Daddy, all the girls wear short dresses now! Barbara wears them, and Linda and Suzie and everyone. . . ." He said, "Barbara and Linda and Suzie and the other girls don't have bodies like yours!" His voice was cold. "No," she said, defying him at last, hating him with all her heart, her voice throbbing, her jaw clenched. He ripped the dress right off her, shredding its delicate fabric. She began to cry, standing there in her white cotton panties. He turned away from her and left the room, throwing the ripped dress at her feet.

Pandora's middle brother killed himself when he was sixteen. Pandora was thirteen. She was the one who found him. She opened the front door and found him in the living room, on the sofa. The gun was in his mouth. He had made a mess. Pandora vomited, and then cleaned up after herself before calling her father at the courthouse. Nobody knew how her middle brother had gotten hold of her father's gun. Pandora's father held her and comforted her all night long. He told her it wasn't her fault. A suicide note was found the next morning on her brother's bureau. The suicide note was incoherent and ranting, declaring that Satan was living in their midst, right in their house, and that Pandora should run for her life, should flee the devil. Her father, who hadn't wept when he saw her brother, wept when he read the note. Later, he threw the note into the fireplace and burned it right in front of Pandora.

When Pandora was a senior in high school, she had a crush on a boy she sometimes saw. Although his father was a banker, he affected a street boy's stance and attitude. When the boy asked her out, Pandora defied her father, who forbid her to date. She agreed to meet the boy at Suzie's house, so her father wouldn't know. She had sex with him the very first time they went out. But she felt nothing, nothing at all during the act, although she yearned to feel something — arousal, contentment, fear, anything at all — but she was numb. In that boy's arms, she had gone somewhere else. Being with him had become a dream. Yet in the midst of that dream she knew exactly what to do to the boy to give him pleasure, although she wasn't sure how she had come to have this knowledge. The boy told his friends about her the very next day. She had sex with the rest of them, one after another, for a period of three weeks, sometimes with two a night, until one of the boy's mothers found out and called Pandora's father and told him.

When Pandora's father got home that night, he made her pull down her panties, and he beat her with a strap. She held in her screams. She didn't want him to see how much he could still hurt her, although a part of her wished she could scream so loud that the whole world would know what he was doing.

The very next day, after her father had left for the court-house, she packed a large bag and took a train to New York. She bought a newspaper in the train station, and by that evening, had found herself the apartment in Times Square and the job at Phone Phantasy-Phun. She was eighteen years old, and she felt very adult; she didn't write or call her father. She did call the boy, the one she'd had the crush on, but he didn't want to talk to her.

Pandora had a very high IQ. She had been told this by her seventh-grade English teacher, who'd heard it from her guidance counselor. The day she learned this, she raced home, proud and eager to tell her father the good news. Her father said, "Don't think you're special just because some old battle-ax of a teacher thinks you are." Pandora learned the next day from her oldest brother that her mother, too, had been extremely smart and had been at the top of her college graduating class, had even written poetry that was published in magazines — before she'd been diagnosed as crazy.

Pandora began to fear that, like her mother, her high IQ would drive her to madness. Already, Pandora secretly suspected that she was crazy, different, not like other people, not really like Barbara and Linda and Suzie, even though they were her very, very best friends. Pandora promised herself that she would never again let anyone know how smart she was, that she would never read or write poetry, or do anything to call attention to her mind, so that her father would never be able to put her in hospital, the way he had to her mother.

In high school, Pandora had been sent to the school psychologist by the principal because her low grades didn't match her high IQ. The school psychologist wore thick glasses, a beard, and a nubby wool sweater with a reindeer design. "Close your eyes," he said, "and imagine that a boy is touching you, fondling you." Pandora, sitting across the room in a leather chair, wearing a plaid jumper, crossed her ankles and did as she was told. "What do you feel?" he asked her. "Nothing," she answered, truthfully. He told her to keep her eyes closed. She heard him rising from his chair, which creaked. He touched her breast through her jumper. "What do you feel now?" he asked. "Nothing," she whispered. He put his hand beneath her skirt, inside her white cotton panties. "And now?" he asked. Although Pandora continued to sit very still and to do as he told her, she didn't answer, because she was no longer really there, no longer in the room with him.

Pandora called her father the day of her nineteenth birthday. She'd been living in New York and working at Phone Phantasy-Phun for a full year. She expected him to yell and scream. Instead, he began to cry, saying he'd missed her and how sorry he was that he'd taken the strap to her that time, and how he wanted her to forgive him, he needed her to forgive him, he'd lost control because he'd been so worried about her, what he had done may have been mis-guided but it was for her own good, and he hadn't deserved to be abandoned by her. He knew she was still a good girl despite what she had done. He'd hired a private detective, but nothing had turned up. He'd feared she was dead. He had nightmares. He couldn't sleep. He was sick with worry.

She agreed, finally, to meet him for lunch. He took the long train ride down to Manhattan. They met at a restaurant she knew, west of Times Square on Tenth Avenue. She wore the only dress she still owned from when she'd lived at home and had been a high school student — it was rayon, with a polka-dot design, and she felt like an imposter in it. Her father walked into the restaurant fifteen minutes late, because his cab driver had deliberately taken a long way around. He looked much older and frailer than when she'd last seen him. He wore bifocals and his nose ran. It broke her heart to see him that way. But she resisted the urge to hold him and com-fort him and say she was coming back home, which was what he wanted. When he asked her how she supported her-self, she said she was a secretary. He offered her money. She refused. She stood and said she had to go. But after that she agreed to have lunch with him every few months.

Her father brought her oldest brother and his wife along to one of their lunches. They met at a French restaurant on the East Side that her brother's wife had seen advertised in a magazine. Pandora felt out of place in such an elegant restaurant. Her brother was now a lawyer in their hometown, living only five minutes from their father. He drank three martinis during lunch, and hardly spoke. Whenever their father said anything, her brother looked away and shut his eyes tight. When Pandora excused herself to go to the ladies' room, her brother's wife followed her. In front of the brilliantly-lit mirror over the sink, as Pandora washed her hands with the restaurant's lavender-scented soap, her brother's wife said angrily, "Your brother is a drunk and a basket case, and I don't know how much more I can take!"

Soon after that lunch, her father died. Her brother called Pandora to tell her. Their father had left most of his money to various charities. Pandora and her brother each received a very small amount. Pandora didn't care. She didn't want his money.

Her brother made all the funeral arrangements. Pandora took the train upstate. Her brother's wife met her at the station, but she and Pandora said nothing to each other during the drive to the funeral parlor. Pandora remained dry-eyed during the entire service. Before she left, she hugged her brother, who was also dry-eyed, and whose breath reeked of alcohol.

A few weeks after the funeral, Pandora remembered for the very first time what used to happen after her father would call to her, "Pandora, Pandora. . . ." She remembered what took place behind those closed doors, in his bedroom, on his bed, beneath his covers, on top of his sheets, in the bathroom, in his car, everywhere. For the first time, she remembered the nightmare of her childhood, the horror that lay at the very core of her being, the horror that had always defined her, that had marked and branded her, although she'd never known it. She screamed. She howled like a beast, wrapping herself in a blanket. She held a razor to her wrists, to her throat. She thought about putting her head in the oven, about running into the streets and jumping off a subway platform. Instead, she lay rigidly on the cold floor of her apartment, willing the memories out of her head, willing them far, far away, willing herself to feel nothing.

About a month later, while she was riding the subway downtown to work, the memories returned. She had convinced herself that she could will them away forever, but now, as she clung to the overhead strap in the crowded, hot subway car, as her body swayed with the subway's movements, she saw that the memories were far more powerful than she, and that they would continue to surface and haunt her whenever they chose—only they didn't feel exactly like memories now, not so distanced, they felt more like visions, hallucinatory visions, like the flashbacks she'd heard that soldiers had after a war. The subway kept lurching, and the flashbacks kept coming, clearer and clearer: "Pandora, Pandora," her father would call. She saw her middle brother touching her while her father stood above them, ordering her brother to touch her harder, harder, and deeper, deeper. When the subway reached her stop, she ran out of the car, onto the platform, and upstairs to the street. She walked the streets of SoHo for an hour until she felt calm enough to step into the offices of Phantasy Phone-Phun, not caring that she'd be docked an hour's pay.

Her first call that night came from one of her regular clients. He wanted Queen Bee to call him filthy names and to tell him over and over how worthless he was. When she was finished with him, another regular client called for Angela. He wanted Angela to wear a frilly, transparent little slip and no panties, and he wanted to tie her by her wrists to a closet door. A third client, a new one, wanted her to listen as he called her a bitch and a whore and a slut.

After work that night, Pandora invited one of the other women, Nilda, out for coffee. She didn't feel ready to go home; she dreaded getting back on the subway. She and Nilda decided to walk uptown to a coffee shop in the West Village. Nilda, who was just five feet tall, always wore very high heels and walked slowly.

While they waited for a light to change on Sixth Avenue, Nilda said, "Pandora is such a different name. Is it real?" Pandora had long ago stopped thinking much about her name one way or another. She figured that Nilda, who'd grown up in a poor village in Puerto Rico, had probably never heard of the myth. Pandora shrugged. "It's real enough," she said, and the light changed.

Because it was three A.M., the coffee shop was filled with hookers, pimps, transvestites, and a few other haunted-looking women who reminded Pandora of herself. Nilda ordered scrambled eggs. Pandora sipped a cup of black coffee. Nilda was sleepy, slightly rambling. She had two kids, and had kicked a major drug habit a few years before. She lived with an aunt in East Harlem who thought she was a private nurse working a late-night shift. Pandora only half-listened to Nilda's complaints about how little they were paid at Phone Phantasy-Phun, and how expensive childrens' clothes were. The flashbacks were threatening to start up again, and Pandora was trying to will them away; at the same time, she longed to confide in Nilda about her father and what he had done to her. But what if Nilda didn't believe that such things could happen, or what if she blamed Pandora? Even though Pandora liked Nilda, she didn't trust her—she didn't really trust a soul in the world—and besides, it wouldn't change a thing either way, whether she told Nilda or not.

Pandora paid the check for both of them. "Catch you tomorrow, Pandora," Nilda said, as they parted outside the restaurant. Pandora almost called her back to tell her, but didn't. Instead, she stepped out into the street and hailed a taxi, dreading too much getting back on the subway while the flashbacks were threatening once again to overtake her.

The phone rang a month later, waking Pandora out of a half-sleep. It was her oldest brother's wife, calling to say that Pandora's brother was dead. "How?" Pandora asked. His wife spoke coldly: "He threw himself off a bridge." Pandora pictured her brother sinking beneath deep black water, helplessly gasping for air.

The flashbacks came again, stronger than ever, as soon as she'd hung up the phone. This time she saw her oldest brother looking sleepy, with his hair all mussed, standing in his pajamas at the foot of their father's bed, watching as her father did something to her that looked like tickling, but wasn't. She heard her father telling her brother to join them in the bed. She wished then, more than anything else in the world, that her oldest brother were still alive. She wanted to tell him that she, too, had remembered, and that she didn't blame him for what their father had forced him to do when he'd been far too young to understand, or to resist.

Pandora took a lover. She had never had one before, hadn't craved sex or intimacy since the day she had run away from home. But now, after her oldest brother's death, sleep came less and less easily to her, and she found herself wanting to be held. Her lover's name was Charlie, and he lived in a studio apartment on the top floor of her building. He was her age, and handsome, with dark hair and a cleft chin. Although he acted in porn movies, he had no illusions of becoming a famous movie star.

One summer night, in Charlie's apartment, after Pandora had cooked dinner for him, and after Charlie had had a few beers, they made love, which had become their usual pattern. As always, Pandora felt neither desire nor arousal during the act, because she saw her father's face, and felt her father's hands upon her skin, even though she knew that it was Charlie lying on top of her, Charlie entering her so forcefully she feared she would split apart and die. She knew, too, how to pretend desire, and she didn't think Charlie suspected.

Afterward, she lay quietly in Charlie's arms. His bed was too narrow for the both of them. It was hot, and the windows were wide open. Pandora's skin was sticky and wet. A radio outside was blasting rap music. But despite everything — her lack of desire, the narrow bed, the heat, and the pounding music — Pandora felt closer to Charlie at that moment than she had ever felt to anyone. He had been her steady, nightly lover for three months; she, who deserved nothing, had been given a gift.

The music outside stopped, and as she lay very still in his arms, almost before she knew she was doing it, she was telling Charlie the truth about her childhood, about her family. At first she spoke hesitantly, but soon her voice grew more forceful. She told him about the suicide of her two brothers, and about how her middle brother had looked when she found him. She told him about the coldness in her oldest brother's wife's voice when she had called with the news of his death.

Pandora also told Charlie about her mother, the naked,

dancing butterfly-lady who had died in hospital, and who Pandora could not forgive. "I believe," she said to Charlie, speaking aloud what she always had been afraid to articulate, even to herself, "that my mother *chose* to go crazy rather than to admit what was happening, rather than to try to rescue her own children." Charlie lay his head upon Pandora's shoulder, and her eyes filled with tears, so that finally she was able to tell him everything, all the terrible things that her father used to do to her after he'd called her into his room. "He was a monster. A *monster*," she repeated. It felt good to say the word aloud to someone else, to shame her father and to lay blame on him, at last.

Pandora described to Charlie the way she felt when the flashbacks came, the way she couldn't breathe and felt as though she would never be able to breathe again. For a long moment, Charlie didn't say anything. Then he said he believed her completely. She was so grateful she lifted up his hand and kissed his fingers one by one — the sort of impassioned, romantic gesture she'd seen actresses make in movies but which she had never before been inspired to make — and she allowed her lips to caress each of his fingers slowly and lovingly.

Pandora wanted to make love again, thinking that perhaps this time she would experience real desire, but Charlie sat up and began complaining about his poorly-maintained apartment and the rough Times Square neighborhood. He told Pandora that he was thinking of moving to L.A., where it was so much warmer and prettier, and where he could live in a house right on the beach.

After Charlie fell asleep that night, the flashbacks came. Pandora bit into her wrist to stifle her sobs, and lay rigidly so as not to disturb and wake him on the narrow bed.

Soon after, Charlie moved to L.A., and Pandora saw no point in taking another lover. She preferred her solitude once again, preferred to be alone with her feelings of self-loathing and shame and rage when the flashbacks came.

During the next few months, Pandora noticed that Nilda was losing a lot of weight. Nilda had also developed a raspy, hoarse cough that wouldn't go away. The doctors finally told Nilda what Pandora had suspected: Nilda had AIDS. Her condition deteriorated rapidly, and very soon she was too weak to come to work.

A timid girl from Korea who wanted to be a fashion designer took Nilda's place at Phantasy Phone-Phun. Pandora missed Nilda. One afternoon, Pandora rode the subway uptown to visit Nilda in the hospital. There were no other visitors. Nilda lay, tiny, shrunken, hairless, covered with sores, almost unrecognizable.

Nilda tried to lift her head to greet Pandora, but couldn't. Pandora reached for Nilda's hand and held it gently, fearing that even normal pressure would break those fragile bones. "I'm so sleepy," Nilda said. Her voice was soft, and Pandora had to lean way down in order to hear her. "Pandora . . . your name is so different . . ." Nilda whispered, and then drifted off to sleep. Pandora continued to sit at Nilda's bedside, continued to hold her wraithlike hand in her own, watching as Nilda slept a troubled sleep. Pandora longed to lie down beside Nilda, longed to share in her pain and her dying. And she saw for the very first time the terrible irony — and the terrible truth — of the myth after which she had been named. She saw that her myth, like all myths, had no real ending, that it was destined to be repeated and repeated, in different guises, forever and ever. She saw that there were girls like herself, and boys like her brothers, all over the world, girls and boys who were destined to remember, and then not to remember, destined to open boxes, and then to close them tight, destined to reach out as far as they could to grasp onto Hope, only to see Hope fly away just beyond their reach, forever and ever.

★ ★ ★

The Mermaid of Orchard Beach

IN SECOND GRADE, MY SECRET FAN-tasy was that one day I would be transformed into a mermaid. I would swim far, far away from the Gun Hill Projects, all the while singing silvery mermaid songs about the sea in an enchanting, melodic voice. In real life, however, I didn't know how to swim, and my singing voice was so off-key that I'd been turned down for the P.S. 41 Glee Club.

I was jealous when Mrs. Washburn, the music teacher who turned me down, accepted Lizzie and Rochelle, my two best friends. When second grade ended, and Lizzie and Rochelle were both sent by their parents to summer camps upstate, far away from the projects, I grew even more jealous.

On a rainy July morning, I stomped angrily into the

kitchen where my mother was washing dishes and listening to Perry Como singing "Catch a Falling Star" on the radio.

"I want to go to camp like Lizzie and Rochelle," I announced.

"We can't afford it." Her voice was flat, and she didn't look up. "You know that."

She was right. I did know that. My father, who drank, had just been laid off again from his job as a TV repairman. This time, he wasn't even looking for another job.

She began to sing along—badly—with Perry Como, and I realized for the first time just whose lousy singing voice it was that I had inherited. This was the last straw: I stomped furiously out of the kitchen and into my bedroom. Throwing myself on my bed, I closed my eyes, fantasizing about the day when I would become a mermaid.

"Lizzie and Rochelle went to camp, so can I hang around with you this summer?" I asked my brother Mike. Mike had just turned fourteen. He was looking at himself in the mirror over his bureau, running his fingers through his brand-new crew cut. Sometimes he and I went to the movies together, or played handball in the playground across the street from the projects.

"Nah, not this summer," he answered, brusquely, surprising me. "I'm gonna go to Orchard Beach every day. You can't hang around with me on the beach." He rolled up the sleeves of his white T-shirt and flexed his muscles. "It ain't personal," he added, still gazing at his own reflection, not seeming to notice when I turned and walked out of his room.

Unlike Mike, my thirteen-year-old sister, Marlene, had never been friendly to me. Nevertheless, after Mike's rejection I approached her. "Forget it, Karen," she said. "I'm going to the beach, like I did last summer." Although Marlene's friends from the projects were all away, too—mostly at bungalow colonies with their families—she had a whole other set of friends at the beach. "You're not going to be *my* problem this summer."

My mother, however, complained that I was staying home too much. "You can't just mope around and daydream all summer long." She'd entered my bedroom without knocking—the room I shared, against my will, with Marlene—interrupting me as I lay in bed, picturing myself floating through the turquoise waters of the ocean, my mermaid hair long and golden, my fish-half sleek and gleaming.

"You need some fresh air, Karen," she went on, sitting on the edge of my bed.

I refused to look at her. Instead, I started to sing "Bless This House," one of the songs the P.S. 41 Glee Club sang at assemblies. I was hoping she'd feel guilty that I had inherited her lousy singing voice.

"I *do* insist upon one thing, Karen," she said, ignoring my singing. "I insist that you start going to the beach with Mike and Marlene."

I shook my head no, still not looking at her. I had no desire to go to Orchard Beach. We'd gone there once together as a family, back when I'd been in kindergarten, during my father's still-sober days. I hadn't liked it: the sun was too hot; my father and mother had argued; and Mike and Marlene had gone off to play handball, telling me I was too little to join them.

"I want you to get some sun," my mother continued. "And I want you to meet other kids your own age. Lizzie and Rochelle aren't the only girls in the Bronx."

This was too much. I finally turned to look at her. "No!"

I shouted. "Just because Daddy got fired, and we're poor and you can't send me to camp like normal parents, why should I do something I don't want to do? I don't *want* to go to the beach with Mike and Marlene!"

"Because," my mother rose from the bed and shouted back even louder, "I'll end up going mad if you don't get out of this apartment! Between you daydreaming in here, and your father passed out on the sofa, I don't have any room to breathe, that's why!"

I shrugged. I refused to shout any longer. My mother's madness wasn't my concern. And although obviously she didn't care, I was slowly going mad myself, ever since school had ended and my two best friends had gone away.

But my mother was adamant. The next morning, she woke me up and sat on my bed as I reluctantly put on the bathing suit she handed me. "Mike and Marlene are waiting for you in the living room," she said. "You stay with them when you get to the beach. Don't wander off, okay?"

I nodded, angrily. Mike and Marlene weren't going to be any happier about this than I was.

In order to get to Orchard Beach, we had to take one bus from Gun Hill Road to Pelham Parkway, and then stand on a long line and wait for a second bus, which was even hotter and more crowded than the first.

Mike, who didn't say a word to me, sat in the back of the bus next to Buddy Boy, a friend of his I'd seen around the projects. Buddy Boy, like Mike, was sporting a new crew cut, and they laughed and flexed their muscles for each other during the ride.

Marlene sat directly across from me. She studied her fingernails, tied and retied the white ribbon that held her bouncy blond ponytail in place, and began applying suntan lotion to her face and neck, even though we hadn't yet stepped out of the bus.

By the time the bus did finally pull into the beach depot, my head ached. In a rush, the passengers — some of whom had been standing the whole way — piled off. They milled around the depot in small groups: mothers counting heads; little kids shouting; babies crying; and everyone gathering up beach bags, towels, blankets, and radios.

Marlene, who was carrying two large terry-cloth beach bags — both with illustrations of girls with bouncy blond ponytails just like her own — spoke to me for the first time that morning. "Don't even think about following me, Karen," she said. "You're too young for my crowd."

Mike, who carried only a small white towel and a radio, left Buddy Boy for a moment and came over to me. "We'll meet up again right here at five o'clock," he said, beginning to look guilty. "You'll be able to find your way back, right?"

I nodded stiffly, staring at the ground.

"Don't be late, Karen," Marlene added. "We may not wait for you if you're late."

"Listen," Mike whispered, leaning over me and looking even guiltier, "if anyone bothers you, I mean, if some jerky guy says anything to you, you just come and get me. I'm at the section where all the bodybuilders hang out. Everyone knows where it is."

"Aay, Mike, come on!" Buddy Boy yelled.

I turned on my heel and began to walk away, although I had no idea where I was going. All I wanted was to get far away from Mike, Buddy Boy, and Marlene. I walked down the staircase leading to the beige-colored sand. I slipped off my white canvas Keds and threw them into my mother's shiny vinyl beach bag, which she'd given me that morning.

I walked barefoot on the sand, past teenaged girls sunbathing in bikinis and groups of boys playing catch. I passed noisy, large families — sometimes two or three families all gathered together on blankets — serving food and drinks to one another, playing cards, listening to music, all looking happier than I remembered my own family ever looking, even during my father's sober days. I didn't stop until I reached the very last section of the beach. Although I was skinny, my legs were strong, and they hadn't grown tired during the long, hot walk.

Unlike the other sections, which were lush with sand, this section was filled with sharp rocks. The water there seemed dangerous: deep and dark, with violent, crashing waves. It suited my mood. I stripped down from my shorts and T-shirt to my bathing suit. I spread my towel on a rock, and sat down.

I remained like that for hours, staring into the water and taking an occasional, reluctant bite of the dry-tasting peanut butter and jelly sandwich my mother had packed for me. Despite the hot sun, I refused to use the suntan lotion she'd also packed.

Finally, I looked at the skinny wristwatch that Lizzie and Rochelle had given me for my birthday. It was time to return to the bus to meet up with Mike and Marlene.

That night, my fair skin turned bright red. I was in so much pain that my mother didn't even yell at me for not using the lotion. Instead, as she rubbed a tingling ointment into my burning skin, she said to my relief, "Okay, no beach for you tomorrow."

But three days later, when my sunburn had healed, she appeared at my bedside, placing the tube of suntan lotion on my pillow.

After that, I took the two buses to Orchard Beach with Mike, Buddy Boy, and Marlene every single day. They ignored me during the ride, and we separated as soon as we arrived at the beach. Then I would walk by myself to that rocky section, which I came to think of as the Faraway Section.

Hardly anyone else ever went to the Faraway Section. Occasionally, there was a teenaged couple making out on one of the rocks. But we just ignored each other, and eventually they would leave, hand in hand, sometimes still kissing as they descended the rocks. Most of the time, though, I sat there all alone, staring out at the ocean, and feeling the heat from the sun on my now-tanned body.

One afternoon, about three o'clock, I was standing on top of a rock, nibbling on my peanut butter and jelly sandwich. I was wearing the only bathing suit I had that summer, a one-piece, green tank suit which my mother had bought for me on sale, when I hadn't been with her to protest. The straps kept slipping off my shoulders, and I kept having to pull them back up.

As I stood there, I saw something way in the distance. I wasn't sure what it was. A large fish? A swimmer? It swam closer and closer, easily riding the big waves, alternating between a breaststroke and a sidestroke. Whatever it was, it swam delicately and yet with great strength. It also looked familiar in some way, as though I'd seen it before. Heart pounding, I climbed a bit farther down the rocks so that I could see it more clearly. By then I had guessed what it was, although I still didn't believe it.

She was fairly close to shore now. Her face shone, and her yellow hair was long and silky. She flipped over and floated on her back. Her tiny, undeveloped breasts glistened in the sunlight. It took me a moment to register that she was about my own age.

The mermaid and I stared at each other. She smiled at me. I managed to smile back. Still smiling, she did a graceful leap and dive, revealing almost in its entirety, her scaley, irridescent, fish-half, which I found just as beautiful as the rest of her. And then she was gone, disappearing somewhere beneath the violent waves of the Faraway Section.

I stood there for a long moment, rocking on the balls of my feet. When I felt steady enough, I climbed all the way down to the shoreline. That way, when she reappeared, I would be even closer to her. I was positive that she would come back, that she would want to see me again as much as I wanted to see her.

I waited, my feet planted firmly in the wet sand, and I took a few more bites of my sandwich, never taking my eyes off the water. I didn't blink or pull up my bathing suit straps when they fell. Then just as I'd known she would, she reappeared, her top half emerging from the water. I stared at her.

She tossed back her long, luxurious, glossy hair. Looking directly at me, she began to sing. Her voice was extraordinary, like some otherworldly, ethereal instrument: soft yet powerful; tremulous yet firm. At first the sound of her voice was so overwhelming that I didn't pay attention to the words of her song. Then I realized it was "Oh Susanna," the very song I'd failed my Glee Club audition by singing.

I took a deep breath, smiled shyly, and joined in, despite my embarrassment at my own out-of-tune voice. But the mermaid nodded encouragingly, and, somehow as we sang, our voices began to harmonize. When we were finished, she threw her head back and laughed, revealing white teeth that glittered like seashells. I laughed too. And then she dove beneath the waves, and was gone.

Although I felt exhilarated, I also felt disappointed. I had wanted to talk to her. I looked at my wristwatch. It was close to five o'clock. Walking the long distance back, I felt weak-kneed. I was over a half hour late.

"I fell asleep in the sun," I lied to Mike and Marlene.

"Well, don't let it happen again," Marlene said. "It's thirty minutes until the next bus."

Mike, standing on line with Buddy Boy, looked guiltier than ever.

My mother, who'd made spaghetti and meatballs for dinner, was annoyed that we were late. Since we'd never told her that I went off by myself, unsupervised, day after day, we couldn't very well say that I had fallen asleep.

"It was the bus, not us." It was Marlene's turn to lie. "It stalled before we got to Pelham Parkway, and we all had to get off and it took forever for the new bus to come."

My mother didn't look convinced, but she didn't say anything else. My father was asleep and snoring loudly on the sofa in the living room. We were all silent as we ate the spaghetti, which my mother hadn't bothered to reheat. Marlene alternated between picking up the cold strands of spaghetti in her fingers and looking at them with distaste, and looking at me across the table with even greater distaste. Mike, who always ate seconds and sometimes thirds at dinner, barely finished his first serving. I finished my entire plate. I was so happy that I didn't care that the food was cold, or that everyone else at the table was angry at me.

The next day, I reached the Faraway Section around noon. I sat on the rock closest to the water. The mermaid appeared moments later. She smiled in greeting, and then immediately began to sing in her astonishing voice, flipping around in the water as she sang, her silver-and-aqua-colored fish-half wet and glowing in the sunlight.

I sat on the edge of the rock singing along with her, swinging my feet and snapping my fingers. We sang for hours: "Grandfather's Clock," "Scarlet Ribbons," "This Land

Is Your Land," "Que Sera, Sera," "Silent Night," and "Home on the Range." Like me, she knew all the words to all of the P.S. 41 Glee Club songs, and we never grew tired or bored.

Over the weeks that followed, as I sang along with the mermaid—who appeared every day, surfacing as soon as she was sure we were all alone — I could hear my own voice changing, growing stronger, more melodious and tuneful. She and I hadn't yet spoken; we hadn't even exchanged names. But that didn't matter. Much more important was the way she and I would sometimes try out something new, a variation on a song that was ours alone. So what if Lizzie and Rochelle had gotten into Glee Club, and so what if they were away at summer camp? I had something neither of them had: a new best friend, and she was a mermaid.

One morning a few weeks later, my mother came into my room. I'd just woken up, and was still beneath the covers. I was surprised to see her at that hour all dressed up, in a flowered, flared shirtdress, with her hair, which she'd recently dyed the same blond color as Marlene's, pinned into a movie star–like French knot. She looked pretty and young, and those things surprised me, too. "I'm liberating you, Karen," she announced, standing over my bed. "No beach today. We're going shopping, just the two of us." She sat on the edge of my bed. "You'll need new shoes for third grade, and I need a few things, too." She sounded almost happy.

Until that moment, I'd blocked out the fact that there were only two weeks left before school started, before my daily trips to the beach stopped. "I don't need new shoes," I said, trying not to reveal my sudden panic. Although I had complained to her more than once about the brown oxfords I'd worn all through second grade, I didn't want to miss a single, precious day with my mermaid, even for a pair of new shoes.

"Karen, your old shoes *are* worn out. You've said so, your-self. And despite the fact that your father isn't working, I'm planning on splurging today. So if I were you, I would take advantage of my *rare* generosity." She smiled and stood up, clearly pleased with herself. "Now go shower and get dressed." She left me alone in the bedroom.

There was no arguing with her. I felt miserable as I waited outside the bathroom until Marlene swept out, still wet from her shower, in her short white terry-cloth robe, with her hair pinned up in the mesh rollers she wore to bed every night.

"I don't want brown shoes this year," I said sullenly, as my mother and I walked up the Fordham Road hill to Alexander's. "I'm sick of brown shoes."

"Nobody said you had to have brown shoes again. You can get black or beige, too. They're both neutral colors."

"I want *turquoise* shoes." Turquoise for the ocean, I thought, although I wasn't going to tell her that.

As we walked, my mother held my hand and swung it, something she rarely did. "Oh, Karen, turquoise hardly goes with anything. You'll never wear turquoise shoes."

"I will *so* wear them. I'll wear them every single day, no matter what."

She didn't say anything more, but she continued to swing my hand. She also hummed tunelessly under her breath. I held my arm stiffly, growing increasingly sullen.

When we reached Alexander's, her first stop was the counter where ladies' scarves were displayed.

"I'm going for bright colors, a new look to cheer me up, not that my husband will even notice," she told the sales-woman, who nodded in sympathy and began placing what seemed like an endless number of long, silky scarves on the countertop. My mother began sorting through them, holding them up to the light, caressing them as though they were precious objects.

I leaned against the counter, shutting my eyes and wishing I were with my mermaid, singing our songs.

"Now it's your turn," my mother said, gaily, after she'd paid for at least five bright red and pink scarves.

Holding my hand again, she led me downstairs to the girls' shoe department. I followed, still feeling sullen, even as she led me to the rack of shoes in my size. And there, in the top row sat a pair of shiny, satinlike turquoise shoes with curled French heels and a T-strap. "Those," I said, pointing, jutting out my chin, preparing for an argument, and hardly believing my eyes.

"They're very pretty," my mother said, to my surprise.

"They *are* pretty," she said again, surprising me even more by taking out her purse and paying for them after I'd tried them on. "And you look so healthy with a tan, Karen," she added, as she led me back out into the street. "Now if only you'd gain a few pounds."

"Thank you for the shoes, really," I said, wondering what had come over her, as we walked back down the hill to the bus stop. She was swinging my hand again.

"You're welcome, really," she said. When we got to the bus stop, she took out the brightest of her bright new scarves and tied it into a pretty bow around her neck without even looking into a mirror, which amazed me as much as anything else she had done that day.

The next morning, I slipped the turquoise shoes into my beach bag. I wanted to show them to my mermaid. I knew she'd love them as much as I did. I waited all afternoon, scanning the water for some sign of her. I was all alone in the Faraway Section, so I couldn't understand why she didn't appear, unless she was angry at me for not showing up the day before. Once she saw the ocean-colored, turquoise shoes, I knew she would forgive me. But she didn't come.

That night, I sat up in bed, watching for the first signs of sunlight through the venetian blinds. "She'll come today," I whispered aloud, softly, so as not to wake Marlene.

"She'll come today," I whispered again, later that morning, after I'd positioned myself on one of the rocks in the Faraway Section. For the first time that summer, the muscles in my calves ached from my long walk on the hot sand. But again she didn't come.

Every day for the next two weeks, I carried the turquoise shoes to and from the Faraway Section with me. And every day I sat there alone, my calves aching, straining to see her among the waves. Sometimes I stood and called out to her: "Hi, it's me, *me*, Karen! Where *are* you?" But she didn't reply, and she didn't appear.

The very last day of summer came, a hazy, humid day, and there was no sign of her. Perhaps her parents had taken her away to some other beach, I told myself — Coney Island, maybe, or Far Rockaway — and so she hadn't had a chance to say good-bye. That must be it, I decided. She *couldn't* have meant to hurt me. Best friends didn't do that to each other.

But the time had come for me to face facts: I wasn't going to see her again. I climbed up to one of the very highest rocks in the Faraway Section, and standing as close to the edge as I dared, with my legs apart, I gazed out into the deep water. I knew what I needed to do: Gathering all my courage, I rocked for a moment on the balls of my bare feet, taking a long, deep breath. At the same instant that a rough, black wave crashed loudly onto a jagged rock below, I began to sing "Scarlet Ribbons," which was her favorite of all our songs.

I sang at the top of my lungs, hoping that wherever she was, no matter how far away, she could hear me. When I finished, I sat down on the edge of the rock, trembling with excitement at the sound of my own voice, which had, over the summer, grown so strong and melodic, more beautiful than the voices of all the girls in Mrs. Washburn's Glee Club — including Lizzie's and Rochelle's — even more beautiful, perhaps, than the voice of my very own mermaid.

A fierce, noisy wind started up, and the sun disappeared behind mean-looking, dark clouds. It began to rain. I stared down at the churning waves below. The wind grew fiercer, the clouds darker, and the rain came down harder. I continued to stand there, letting the cold raindrops splatter on my skin.

I felt powerful and inviolate, understanding for the very first time all that I had accomplished that summer. I had created a mermaid, shiny, turquoise shoes, a powerful and stunning singing voice, and a lively, generous mother who'd taken me shopping and held my hand and laughed and sang. I had done all *that,* all by myself — created so much from what was really so very little.

As suddenly as it started, the rain tapered off to a cool drizzle, and I walked slowly back to the bus depot to meet up with Mike and Marlene for the very last time that summer, knowing that nobody, but *nobody*, could take away from me these things that I had created. Not then, and not ever.

★ ★ ★

Gypsy Lore

"**H**E COMES IN. HE GOES OUT. HE comes in and he goes out. That's all," the Gypsy said.

Anna listened and played with the topaz birthstone ring her parents had given her two years before, on her thirteenth birthday. She'd first met the Gypsy one July afternoon when she was shopping in midtown for a bikini, which she'd never bought, because she felt too flat-chested. She'd grown hungry, and she saw a sign: GYPSY FORTUNE TELLER. LUNCH AND SUPPER SERVED. Anna went upstairs. The room was dark and gloomy, and there were no other customers. The Gypsy sat alone at a large table. Against the wall were some folding chairs.

Anna stood in the doorway and stared. The Gypsy was bald in spots and had sparse yellow hair. She wore a cotton kerchief

with a gaudy floral design, but it was falling off. She was haggard and heavily made-up. Her earrings were black plastic
squares with red, shiny triangles hanging on the bottom.

"May I see a menu?" Anna asked.

"You want egg salad or tuna fish?" the Gypsy replied. She
sounded tired.

Last year, right before her fourteenth birthday, Anna had
gotten food poisoning from bad mayonnaise. "Neither, then.
Just my fortune." She hoped that the Gypsy wasn't offended.

The Gypsy told Anna's fortune with cards. "One day soon
you'll go to Europe or maybe California. You'll go to a big
entertaining, too."

"An entertaining?"

"A party. You'll go to a big party," the Gypsy explained, as
Anna handed her ten dollars.

Anna went back every week. She didn't believe a word
that the Gypsy said, but she went back anyway. Every
Saturday morning she joined three old women there. None
of them ever spoke to her. But the Gypsy liked Anna and
always took her last so that they could talk. "Annie," she
would say, "you're a young girl. I only wish I were so young.
Marry rich. Don't go for love. Just money."

On Saturday afternoons, Anna took an art course. She was
frustrated. "You must learn to *see,*" the instructor would
frown. "Is that what the model looks like?" Anna looked at
what she had drawn: The boy in the dream that she'd had the
night before.

Anna had two real girlfriends. Anna liked Mindy best, but
she was away, working as a counselor at a summer camp.
Barbara, who was home, wore pigtails and cute dotted swiss
blouses, and her voice was loud. Barbara had been seeing a
boy steadily for the last two years. Barbara wasn't a virgin.
"I've been doing it with Joe for a year, I guess," she'd told

Anna. "You don't know what you're missing." But Anna wasn't envious of Barbara because Joe, Barbara's boyfriend, had bad breath.

Barbara got Anna a date with Peter, one of Joe's friends, although Anna hadn't asked her to.

They went out on a double date. Peter chain-smoked and had dirty fingernails. "Do you smoke?" he asked Anna.

"No." Silently, she added, "I hate you. Go away."

They were in a movie theater. He put his hand on Anna's thigh. She had worn a new dress just in case he turned out to be cute. She removed his hand. A few minutes later he put it back, even higher. Barbara and Joe were kissing and Anna could hear Joe breathing. She could imagine how bad his breath was just from the sounds he made. The movie was about a mother of two who falls in love with her husband's psychiatrist. Anna felt that she understood the tormented actress with her frightened, sensual eyes. Peter left his hand on Anna's thigh for the rest of the movie. He didn't move his fingers up and down or rotate them along her stocking. His hand just remained there — menacing and greasy. After the movie, they went to an ice-cream parlor that boasted waitresses in red leotards. Peter kept saying, "I'm gonna pinch one, I swear."

Barbara laughed. "Let's see."

Peter was eating a chocolate sundae. Some of it dripped on his chin.

Anna was sickened. "You have stuff on your chin."

Peter was embarrassed and wiped it off with Anna's napkin.

Anna told the Gypsy about Peter. "He tried to unhook my bra later at Joe's house."

The fortuneteller shook her head. "Don't let him do that. Not him. He knows nothing. That's not the way."

One day, Anna bought the Gypsy a gift: a box of chocolate-covered cherries. The Gypsy kissed her cheek and laughed. "Annie," she said, "you are like these chocolates, so innocent." She and Anna finished the box of chocolates together. Finally, Anna said, "What's it like?"

The Gypsy laughed very hard. "I'll tell you. He comes in and goes out. That's it."

Anna made her repeat it again. "Tell me more," she insisted.

"There's not much more. First it's some kissing. You know how to kiss already. That much you know. Then you touch each other. Then you touch each other some more. Then he comes in. That's it, Annie. The whole thing. There's not so much to it. That's why you should marry for money."

"Sometimes I dream that I'm doing it," Anna pleaded. "But I can't imagine what it feels like. *Really* feels like. Inside and all."

The Gypsy shook her head. "Stop, Annie. You embarrass me. One day soon enough you'll see and then Big Deal. You'll see."

Anna went to the beach one Sunday with a girl that she knew slightly, whose parents were friends of Anna's parents. Karen went often and had a deep tan. Anna felt conspicuous in her whiteness. Two boys sauntered over. "Hi. You girls want company?" Karen made room for them on the blanket. The boys had a blaring radio with them. They placed it on the blanket and sat down. "Where are you girls from?"

"Deer Park." Karen crossed her legs. "You boys come here a lot?"

"Yeah. A lot." They were both very tanned. One was named Kevin and one was named Ronnie. Anna put on a big smile and told them about her art class. Kevin seemed bored, but Ronnie said, "I used to draw, too. Real wild things. My mother was scared of my drawings."

Anna thought maybe she liked Ronnie. He held her hand. Kevin announced that he and Karen were going for a walk. Ronnie and she listened to music until they came back. Karen was flushed, and she tried to mouth some words to Anna, but Anna couldn't understand. "Our turn to take a walk," Ronnie said. Anna rose and followed him, wishing she'd bought that bikini after all. Her modest two-piece bathing suit seemed dowdy.

She and Ronnie walked to a section of the beach that was rocky and deserted. He leaned over and kissed her. Her toes curled in the sand, and for the first time she thought maybe she was excited. She pressed herself against him and he pushed her down, awkwardly. He fell on top of her. He put his hand inside her bathing suit top. She rubbed his neck, because Barbara had once told her that Joe always got hard when she did that to him. Anna kept rubbing his neck. He put his hand on her stomach. She felt excited, but frightened, too. What if he put his hand in the bottom of her suit? What if he had a condom with him, and wanted to go further? She felt his hand sliding downward. Should she keep rubbing his neck? His hand was inside. She closed her eyes and tried to focus: She imagined that his hand was a foreign traveler with a French accent and that her body was an unfamiliar country. It made the roving fingers feel less like roving fingers. She wanted to be thrilled, to feel joyous, but she felt ticklish instead. "Stop," she said, softly, trying to sound sensual, not scared. His hand slowly emerged. He sat up, his face was sweating. Anna felt proud, and she kissed him lightly, just for an instant. He took her phone number and they walked back to the blanket.

Anna and Karen went to the movies the next day.

"Do you like Kevin?" Anna asked Karen as the woman with the flashlight passed their row.

"I think so. He's a great kisser. And he's cute, especially with that little beard he's growing. Do you like Ronnie?"

"Yes." She paused. Karen seemed to expect more. "He's also a great kisser."

The next week, Peter called. "No, I can't see you again," she told him. "I have a boyfriend now." Actually, Ronnie hadn't even called yet.

Anna missed the next Saturday at the art school and the Gypsy's. Her mother's cousin had a family gathering in Woodmere and Anna's mother insisted that she come. Anna wore an outfit that her mother had picked out for her: blue leggings and an oversize sweater that was much too big and kept sliding off her shoulders. Her thirteen-year-old cousin Bill, who wore braces, asked her to dance. She said she had a sprained ankle, and she sat with her parents. She drank too much of her father's red wine and felt sick. Her mother had to give her Alka-Seltzer when they got home.

The Gypsy opened her door late the following Saturday morning. Anna and the three old women waited together on the staircase. Anna was silent, and the women talked among themselves. Finally, the Gypsy appeared. She wore a paisley kerchief on her head, and a pair of green, swishing earrings that Anna had never seen before. The three women had their fortunes told. Anna heard the Gypsy say to one of them, "Your son is fine. He hasn't written because he's been busy. You'll hear from him very soon. And he'll have good news for you."

Anna didn't listen any more until it was her turn. She had meant to buy the Gypsy some more chocolate candy but had forgotten.

"So what happened last week, Annie? Because I have a great surprise for you." The Gypsy spoke with more animation than usual. Her green earrings swished loudy. "My nephew just arrived from Hungary. He's eighteen. He's staying with me now, in my apartment downtown, and he'd like to make friends. I told him all about you. You don't have to date him. Just show him around the city a little bit." She took Anna into the back room, where Anna had never been before. It was half-kitchen, half-bedroom.

A good-looking boy sat on the bed. He was dark and had the beginnings of a mustache. His clothes weren't stylish but he looked romantic in his beige turtleneck and navy blazer. He greeted Anna with a smile and a thick accent. Anna sat down next to him on the bed. The Gypsy sat on his other side. The three of them ate tuna fish sandwiches.

"You like it here?" Anna asked.

"So far." He smiled again.

"He's only been here a week, Annie," the Gypsy said, standing. "Give him time to decide."

The boy laughed.

Anna wasn't sure how well he understood what was being said. "I have to go," the Gypsy said. "I have customers."

Anna and the boy went for a walk. "Where do you and your aunt live?" She realized that she didn't know where the Gypsy's apartment was.

"Twenty-third Street," he said. "The eastern part."

Without speaking, they walked toward the Gypsy's apartment. Anna had already missed part of her art class and she felt guilty. Her mother would shout, "What am I paying good money for if you're going to take off whenever you feel like it?" But Anna didn't care: Being with this boy was so much more exciting than standing in a drafty room in front of an easel.

As they crossed Third Avenue, Anna said, "You see that hot dog man? That's a New York specialty."

The boy glanced at the fat man and his hot dogs. He

smiled vaguely, and Anna wondered again how much he understood of what she said to him.

He had a key to the Gypsy's apartment. The apartment wasn't what she'd expected: no wild fabrics; no exotic music; no dancing sisters and uncles. The living room was bright and modern, with an orange sofa, a large TV, an Elvis clock, and a photograph of a young, blond woman holding a plump baby in her arms. Anna turned away from the photo.

The boy went into the kitchen and came back sipping from a can of Pepsi. She walked toward him. "I'd like a sip." He understood immediately and handed her the can. She barely tasted it. She sat down on the sofa, delighting in the vibrancy she felt. The boy seemed to sense it, and sat down beside her.

Anna was conscious of her every move. She threw her arms around the boy's neck and kissed him. His tongue felt like a fuzzy peach. He began to pant. She rubbed his neck. He panted harder. Anna lay down. "No mind, just body," she whispered. The boy looked up. "Nothing," she said. She got bored. She moved his hands all over her body but was dissatisfied. She sat up. "Listen. I'll sleep with you."

The boy's eyes were closed. "Okay," he said.

Anna got undressed and left her clothes on the floor. She stared at him. He was thin and wiry. His eyes were still closed. She wasn't quite ready yet. She removed her topaz birthstone ring and placed it inside her pocketbook. Then she was ready, and she walked to the boy, wondering idly where the Gypsy thought they were.

And then the boy was everywhere, all at once. She, too, closed her eyes. It hurt a little, but not for long. He seemed to know what to do, how to move, how to touch her breasts and her belly while he moved himself, faster and faster inside her. It seemed like one of her dreams: imagined; vague; unreal.

He sat up. "I love you," he said. His voice was hoarse.

Anna stared at the ceiling. The Gypsy had been right, after all: in and out and at last, finally over.

She wished she had gone to art class.

★ ★ ★

Making Love, Making Movies

JEFF WAS A HAPPILY MARRIED, SUCCESS-
ful Hollywood screenwriter. Sasha, his wife, was an actress,
mostly doing TV commercials in which she'd been typecast
as a happy homemaker type, espousing the delights of
laundry detergents and spaghetti sauces.

Jeff was meeting with a producer to discuss his latest
script, *The Junkie and the Lady,* about a heroin addict from
New York City's Little Italy — a young Al Pacino type —
who falls in love with a haughty European countess — a
young Ingrid Bergman type. The producer and he were discussing the best way to give the script an upbeat, positive
ending. This didn't bother Jeff at all, since he'd long ago
given up any illusions about art and integrity. Screenwriting

was a job, that was all. A job that was more lucrative than some.

After the meeting, the producer took him out for a drink, along with a blond, blue-eyed, pink-lipsticked actress named Bambi. Jeff had met plenty of girls just like Bambi before: a few years out of Hollywood High, not too bright, more starstruck than talented. Bambi was a living, breathing Hollywood cliché, the kind of girl who probably drew a heart over the *i* in her name. Why he went back with her to the house in Silver Lake that she shared with three other blondes, he had absolutely no idea. All he knew for sure, as he lay on Bambi's waterbed, waiting for her to come out of the bathroom where she'd gone to "change into something more comfortable," was that, after ten faithful years of marriage, he was about to betray Sasha.

Bambi emerged from the bathroom in a short black lace nightie. She climbed on top of him. He closed his eyes and inhaled her rose-scented perfume. "This isn't real," Jeff thought, as he felt her tongue exploring his chest. He felt bewildered, a Jack Lemmon type. "This is just a movie," he thought, "one I could write in my sleep, it's so cliché-ridden." After they made love, Bambi sat bolt upright, her eyes glowing. She spoke passionately, her tiny nostrils flaring with emotion. "Everyone else thinks Marilyn Monroe was so great. But not me. I think Jayne Mansfield was greater."

That was it, Jeff realized, the perfect last line of this movie, which, he decided, would be called *Bambi and the Screenwriter.* And which, he reminded himself, had nothing to do with his real life.

When Jeff returned home that night, Sasha was curled up on the sofa in her lavender terry-cloth bathrobe, eating raspberry ice cream directly from the container, and watching *The Year of Living Dangerously* on the VCR.

"Sorry I'm late," Jeff said, after she'd put the movie on pause, "but the damned meeting took forever."

"Ummn," she said, looking up and licking her spoon. He waited for her to rise up and throw her ice cream in his face, to call his bluff, to say that she knew all about him and Bambi. But that would have been a scene from another movie. In this movie, as the unsuspecting wife, she simply turned the VCR back on. "Look at her," she pointed at the screen, "just look at that woman." Her voice was thick with envy.

He knew what she meant. Sasha had a thing about Sigourney Weaver. She watched her movies constantly. She was wildly jealous of her. Sigourney Weaver had never had to make TV commercials, Sigourney Weaver had never gotten typecast as the All-American Happy Housewife. Sigourney Weaver, Sasha believed, had it all. "Just look at her," she sighed.

Jeff looked at the screen. The charismatic, blue-eyed Mel Gibson was kissing the charismatic, dark-eyed Sigourney Weaver.

"I mean, here she's doing a socially-conscious romantic drama," Sasha said, with great envy and bitterness, "and in *Ghostbusters* she did light, hip comedy. I mean, that woman can do anything, anything at all." Sasha felt that, given half a chance, she, too, could do anything. Jeff knew this wasn't true. Sasha was acting to full capacity in the TV commercials she made. But that didn't make him love her any less. The girl he'd fallen in love with during sophomore year at UCLA had never been destined for stardom, and he liked it that way.

That night, as he lay in bed next to Sasha, he felt a pang of guilt over his *Interlude with Bambi* — another possible title for the movie — but he reminded himself that he had nothing to feel guilty about. Because it hadn't been real. It had just been some silly Grade-B movie. He did understand, of course, that his guilt was causing him to think absurd things, but it worked. He felt better. He felt absolved. If he could make moviegoers believe that a European countess could fall in love and live happily ever after with a dope addict from Little Italy, he could make himself believe in his own innocence.

The next time it happened, about a month later, it was with a forty-five-year-old brunette whom he'd met at the dry cleaners. He found himself striking up a conversation with her, complimenting her on the long green velvet party dress she'd just had dry-cleaned. He helped her carry the dress out to her car. They stood together in the parking lot, where she informed him almost immediately that she was divorced and bored. She was another movie cliché, he thought. A different one than Bambi. A Lauren Bacall type, with a husky, cigarette-scarred voice. Her name was Lorelei, as perfect a name for her role as Bambi's had been for hers.

At Lorelei's invitation, Jeff followed her in his car back to her large, luxurious house in Bel Air. A mustached gardener was working outside. Inside, she mixed him a martini, straight up, with three olives. He'd become Bogie to her Bacall. "It's just a movie," Jeff thought, as he and Lorelei made a hungry kind of love on her king-size bed. The movie would be titled, simply, *Affair,* and it would end the following way: The screenwriter breaks off the affair. The divorcée takes an over-dose of sleeping pills. The screenwriter finds her passed out in her bedroom. He drives her to the hospital, her stomach is pumped, and she understands, finally, that their affair, which can lead nowhere, must come to an end. And now, with that knowledge, she can go on happily with the rest of her life. Jeff rolled off Lorelei. He looked up at the ceiling.

"What are you thinking about?" Lorelei asked, lighting a cigarette.

"The movies," Jeff answered.

"Oh, the movies," she said, in that husky voice, taking a dramatic, Tallulah Bankhead—like drag on her cigarette, "are absolute crap. But I adore them." She paused, blew out some smoke. "Doesn't everybody?"

When Jeff got home that night, Sasha was watching Sigourney Weaver on a PBS TV special. "I can't believe this," she said plaintively to Jeff, before he'd even taken off his new denim jacket, "she can even do intellectual, avant-garde stuff!"

The third time was with another screenwriter, Molly Smith, a woman he'd known for years. Molly was cute, with her cropped dark hair, her black leather pants, and her huge, dangling earrings. Her husband was an actor. That afternoon, Jeff ran into her in a Mexican restaurant, where he was eating a burrito and doing revisions on *The Junkie and the Lady.* Molly was at the next table, doing revisions on her own script, a tearjerker about an estranged mother and daughter who are reunited after twenty years. "It's called *Friends Again,*" she told Jeff. Jeff and Molly drank frozen margaritas, discussed happy endings, and then went off together to the studio apartment Molly kept in West Hollywood.

Jeff respected Molly, he could really care about her. After they'd made love, she immediately stood up, slipped into her black leather pants and black T-shirt. She leaned over and kissed him full on the mouth. "You know," she said, in a courageous, emotion-filled voice, "it was wonderful — so wonderful — but we must never, never do this again!"

Somberly, he nodded. He knew she was right. Oh, it was painful, but she was right. This was a different movie, called *Love and Pain.* He felt like a serious British actor, an Albert Finney type. And she was a Vanessa Redgrave type. They were playing the parts of a man and a woman who must sacrifice their love for the sake of their long-standing marriages. *For the sake of our kids,* he thought. Although, of course, neither he and Sasha, nor Molly and her husband, had any kids.

When he got home, Sasha was watching Sigourney Weaver in *Alien.* "Damn," she cried out, near tears, "just damn her! She can do action-packed sci-fi, too!"

The fourth time, on a rainy afternoon, he spent a long, languorous afternoon in bed in a pink house in Beverly Hills with Dora, the wife of the producer of *The Junkie and the Lady.* The producer was away on business. Dora was bright, funny, and extremely talkative, a Carrie Fisher type. He felt manly and taciturn around her, a Tom Selleck type.

Afterward, Jeff was supposed to meet with the son of a college friend who wanted advice on how to get his first script, *Love in an Orange Grove,* produced. Suddenly feeling tired, Jeff called his friend's son from Dora's bedroom and canceled the meeting. He just wanted to go home, take a hot bath, and fall asleep. Although lately, when he slept, his dreams disturbed him. They had turned into bona fide, feature-length movies, starring real actors and actresses, with credits and coming attractions and warnings about not smoking. He always awoke confused. There were no longer any boundaries he could count on. Dreams, movies, life: They were becoming one.

He drove home in the pouring rain, nearly getting into two accidents on the freeway. He walked in the front door, and found Sasha on the sofa. She was wearing a tight black jersey jumpsuit he'd never seen her wear before, with her hair pulled severely back in a style he'd also never seen her wear before. She was locked passionately in an embrace with a man he'd never seen before, either, a Mel Gibson type, with rugged good looks and intense blue eyes. Somehow, Sasha had transformed herself into a Sigourney Weaver type. With her tight jumpsuit and her severe hairstyle, she looked fierce and intelligent and sexy all at once, an actress who could do an avant-garde film on Monday, a flip comedy on Tuesday, a sci-fi flick on Wednesday, a romantic drama on Thursday. . . . Yet, this wasn't the real Sigourney Weaver. This was Sasha, his wife, who did TV commercials about spaghetti sauce. And who was cheating on him.

Jeff just stood there, staring at the Sigourney Weaver type and the Mel Gibson type, who were both staring back at him. Nobody said a word. It was a long freeze shot, rich with emotion and pain. Jeff understood, at that epiphanous moment in the movie, that he'd been wrong to think that their whole lives could revolve around sham and illusion without their having to pay for it. Life, like most movies — even the trashiest ones — had a moral ending. "Ye shall reap what ye shall sow": He could picture one of those cantankerous old character actors, a Walter Brennan type, saying this and wagging his finger in Jeff's face.

Silently, Jeff turned away from the scene before him. He walked outside and stood on the lawn, hanging his head, getting soaked in the rain. How he yearned for this movie, *Life,* to have an upbeat, positive ending. He yearned to be a Gene Kelly type, singing and dancing in the rain. But he was no song-and-dance man. No, he was a miserable man, getting drenched by the rain, a man who cheated on his wife, a man who was cheated upon by his wife, a man who cheated the moviegoing public by turning out crap. He was a lonely man, scared of his own dreams. His life was empty.

He looked up into the sky. Through the rain, through the lightning and thunder, the HOLLYWOOD sign, high in the hills, shone out at him like a beacon. And, at that moment, what he read into the sign was this: NO, NO, DON'T DESPAIR, YOUR LIFE IS NOT EMPTY! He shivered in the cold rain, but he felt better, too: no longer jealous, no longer angry, no longer sad. Everything was going to be alright. Creating illusions for people, providing them with happiness — however fleeting and formulaic — was no crime against humanity. Rather, it was an act of love: he loved the movies, he loved the scripts he wrote for the movies, he loved the moviegoing public, and he loved all the movie stars, Sigourney Weaver and Mel Gibson and Albert Finney and Walter Brennan and Jayne Mansfield and Jack Lemmon and all the rest of them. He loved Bambi and Lorelei and Molly and Dora. And he loved Sasha, oh, how he loved her. And Sasha loved him. Despite the fact that they had both strayed. Naturally, they had strayed. He should have expected it all along. What kind of a movie would it be if they hadn't, if there were no conflicts, no guilt, no angst, no dark nights of the soul? All of the interesting characters in the movies, the ones with any depth and passion, had moments of weakness, had moments when they strayed from the righteous path. Without sin, without redemption, there would be no movies. So what if the movies were filled with lies? The lies were the means to an end. And the end was this: true love would win. It always did. It had to. That was the way it was in Hollywood. And he loved Hollywood!

And because his love was so great, so powerful, he kicked his heels, did a little soft-shoe, and, before he knew it, he was singing in the rain, just singing, dancing, and weeping in the rain.

★ ★ ★

The Murder of
Juanita Appel

T HE LITERARY EXCHANGE OCCU-
pied two floors of a small, barely noticeable office
building squeezed between a parking garage and a vacant lot
on Amsterdam Avenue. I was there to attend the first
meeting of Juanita Appel's writing class. A dozen of us —
mostly males, like myself — were sitting around a large
wooden table in a conference room that had seen better
days. I felt self-conscious: fresh out of college, boyish and
blond, still fighting an occasional outbreak of adolescent
acne, the youngest person in the room.

It was a hot, rainy night. The air conditioner was broken,
and the ceiling was leaking. A puddle was forming on the
floor. Juanita Appel, our teacher, was nowhere in sight.

From the conversations going on around me, I gathered that the workshop was divided roughly in half: those who were Juanita Appel's admirers, members of a fierce, but tiny, cult; and those, like me, who'd never even heard of her before they'd registered for the class. I had only Wednesday nights off from my job selling encyclopedias by phone, and Juanita's was the only class offered on Wednesdays. And since I intended to become a best-selling novelist as quickly as possible, I'd gone ahead and registered.

While we were sitting around waiting for Juanita to show up, I noticed that the guy on my left, who sported a pencil-thin gray mustache and a black patch over his right eye, had placed one of Juanita's novels on the table in front of him. The title was spelled out in fiery red letters: *Dancing Loving Dreaming of the Air Mountains Sea*. "Excuse me," I said, tapping him on the shoulder, trying to make my voice sound older and deeper, "I'm not familiar with Juanita's work. May I have a look?"

Sneering, he handed the book to me, letting me know how little he thought of anyone not familiar with Juanita's work.

Ignoring his sneer, I looked for her author photograph on the back cover, but there was none. Instead, there were blurbs from a bunch of obscure-sounding writers, all of whom had foreign names. "Juanita Appel is a brilliant surrealist," Vladamir Goranoffski declared. "A magical realist with an erotic streak a mile wide," gushed Miguel "Pocho" Echeverria.

I didn't bother reading any more of the blurbs. I looked at her bio: "Juanita Appel was born in the banana country of Colombia, South America. She spent her childhood back and forth between that country and the Bronx, New York." It also gave her birth date. I did some quick math; Juanita was forty — no spring chicken.

I was glancing over the list of the other books she'd written, when the mustached student deigned to look over at me with his left eye. "None of her books are even in print," he said, with a cold rage in his voice, as though I were to blame for what he clearly saw as a terrible injustice.

I didn't respond. I was too depressed at the thought that this out-of-print, surrealist writer was the person from whom I'd hoped to learn how to become a best-selling, megabuck-making novelist.

I read the first sentence of the novel, and grew even more depressed. I liked straightforward stuff. Not this female Latin/Bronx sexed-up pseudo-Kafka with her convoluted prose about rainbow-colored parrots hanging from trees while quoting Samuel Beckett and devouring pistachio nuts swollen like vulvas. I slammed the book shut. Writers like Juanita stayed poor and obscure. I decided that I would drop out after the first class session, and demand a full refund. I handed the book back to the mustached student, who adjusted his eyepatch and sneered at me again.

Finally, Juanita Appel arrived, twenty minutes late. She hovered in the doorway for a moment, staring impassively at us. She was at least six feet tall. Her skin was bronze; her eyes pale blue; her lips a pink so pale they bordered on white. Her thick, wavy chestnut hair fell to her waist, and she wore a clinging black dress that came to her ankles.

Without apologizing for her lateness, she entered the classroom, taking long, graceful strides to avoid the puddles. Seating herself with regal posture at the head of the table, she looked up at the dripping ceiling. Her voice was soft but strong. "Go home, send me your stories during the week, and we'll discuss them next time. Any questions?" Her accent was a curious combination of elegant Spanish and tough Bronx.

There were no questions. Her fans seemed overjoyed just being in her presence, breathing the same air she breathed. The others seemed too bewildered to ask anything. I, too, couldn't speak. I could barely think. To my complete shock, I—who'd barely even noticed the girls in my classes during my four years of college—had fallen head over heels in love with Juanita Appel.

I lingered outside the building, waiting for her to come out. Discreetly, I followed her to the bus stop. Although I lived only a few blocks from the Literary Exchange, in an apartment on Columbus Avenue that my parents were helping me to pay for, I also followed her onto the downtown bus.

Taking a risk, I sat directly across from her. Maybe she would be pleased to see me. I would tell her I was on my way to meet a friend at a West Village café. I would invite her along. We'd sit together in a dark, smoky corner, sipping espresso. After a few minutes, I would excuse myself and pretend to telephone my friend, who would have met with an unexpected emergency and wouldn't be able to join us. Then I would be alone with Juanita Appel, the woman who had stolen my heart. But that didn't happen. She didn't even notice me.

She got off at the very last stop. Although it was growing dark, the rain had stopped, and the West Village streets were crowded. With a racing heart, I followed behind her. She stopped at a greengrocer. The sight of her choosing among the bin of swollen, hot pink grapefruits made me weak with desire. She paid for two grapefruits and then continued on, swinging the greengrocer's plastic bag as she walked.

Near the corner of Sixth Avenue, she pulled a metal key ring from her pocket and opened the door of a nondescript building across the street from a shop that sold kinky sexual devices, and next door to a tiny restaurant known for its varieties of bagel sandwiches. Without turning around, she disappeared inside. I stood outside her building for hours in the darkness, craning my neck, trying to figure out which window was hers, and wondering how I would survive until the next Wednesday.

The following week, the class was smaller. Only her fans had returned. While waiting for her, they argued about "subtext" and "intentionality" in her work. The mustached fellow, whose patch was over his left eye this time, argued the loudest. I didn't join in their conversation. Instead, I sat there wondering what Juanita would do if she knew that all week long, between my telemarketing stints, I had wandered back and forth in front of her building. I'd also wandered in and out of the kinky sex shop across the street until the proprietor became suspicious and I felt obligated to buy a black leather mask. And I'd sat in the bagel place next door to her building, composing a short story for her class on a legal-size yellow pad, hoping she'd come through the door. I had eaten bagels with jam, with butter, cheddar cheese, roast beef, and sturgeon slices until I'd wanted to throw up. But I hadn't seen Juanita once, not even from afar.

At last, again twenty minutes late, Juanita came through the door of the conference room. This time she was wearing a short, strapless red dress that showed off her full, round breasts, her narrow waist, shapely calves, and strong ankles. It was raining again, and as she stepped over the puddles, I caught a glimpse of bronzed inner thigh.

She sat down, appearing unfazed by the reduced size of the class. With no preliminaries, she began to discuss our stories. She read sections of them aloud, and it soon became apparent to me that all the other students were trying to mimic her style. "I'm sure that you meant well," she would say listlessly to each student, "but this just wasn't written from the heart." Eager to please her, the student would nod vehemently, "You're right, Juanita, not from the heart! Next time, definitely, from the heart!"

Juanita would sigh, moving on to the next story, continuing to speak softly, occasionally licking her pale lips. Sometimes her Colombian accent dominated; sometimes her Bronx. She seemed utterly bored.

At the end of the class, she said, "Okay, send me more of your stuff for next time."

I felt stricken and ashamed. I was the only student whose work hadn't been discussed. I rose along with the others, keeping my head down.

As I was walking out the door, I heard her speak my name. "Please," she said, wearily, "remain after class a moment."

When all the other students had gone, I stood before her.

"Listen," she said, remaining seated at the table, and looking up at the ceiling, "I don't think this is the right class for you. Maybe you could transfer to Margot Madd's class. Or Bill Smith's. Did you know they both teach here?" She looked at me hopefully.

I nodded. I knew they both taught there, although neither on Wednesdays. Originally, Margot Madd and Bill Smith had been the writers I'd most wanted to study with; after all, they were both famous and they both wrote about real life. I'd read Margot's novel, *At Play,* about a rich girl whose parents neglect her, and who develops a cocaine habit, and I'd found it both sexy and moving. Bill Smith had written lots of novels, and they were all deep and brutal, about men who drank a lot and got into fistfights. But I no longer wanted to study with either of them. I wanted only Juanita. "No," I answered weakly, "I can't."

Juanita picked up the loose pages of *One Night at a Bar in Philly*, my story. "It's really not my kind of thing," she said. "I can't be of help to you."

I dropped to my knees in front of her.

Her pale blue eyes widened.

"I love you," I said pleadingly, looking up at her. A lock of my hair fell into my eyes. I was sweating.

"Hey, is this some kind of sick joke or what?" she demanded angrily, in her Bronx accent.

I shook my head. "I love you," I repeated stubbornly, pushing my hair from my eyes so that I could look directly up into her dark, exotic face. "I must make love to you tonight or I'll die!"

"Whoa, calm down." Her voice became maternal and kind. She rose from her chair and stood. She looked down at me from her great height. "How old are you?"

"Twenty-two," I mumbled, realizing for the first time that I was just a child in her eyes. I felt humiliated.

"Why, you're just a boy, just a child," she said, echoing my thought.

Tears filled my eyes.

"Get up, *pobrecito*," she said softly in her Colombian accent.

I got up from the floor, the knees of my blue jeans wet from the puddle in which I'd been kneeling. I stood before her. To my astonishment, she pushed me down onto the top of the wooden table. I began to tremble. She lay on top of me. Her red dress rustled as it slid up her thighs. "*Ay, Dios mio*, such a young and pretty boy!" she cried, sounding very Spanish and very hot-blooded.

From that moment on, Juanita and I had a sex life that knew no bounds, no inhibitions. We were insatiable. I loved to lick and bite and stroke her body's every nook and cranny, and she did the same to me. But despite my taste for her flesh, I just couldn't develop a taste for her writing. At first I didn't let on. I was so grateful, so amazed, that she loved me. I couldn't believe my luck as she fell into my arms night after night, her muscular, lithe body resting beside mine.

After a few weeks, however, I grew bold. Despite our age difference, despite the fact that I was her student, I became increasingly forward in my objections to her work. "I'm just a simple guy," I would tell her, after we'd made love in the creaky loft bed in her tiny, dark studio apartment overlooking a back alley, "like most people. But simple doesn't mean dumb, if you know what I mean."

"No, my little darling," she would answer, lying back and playing with her nipple in the way she knew never failed to arouse me, "I don't know what you mean."

"I mean, I don't go for all these arty inventions of yours. You've lived a fascinating life, Juanita. Write about real life. *Your* real life."

"What is 'real life,' my darling?" She played teasingly with her other nipple.

I turned away, growing impatient with her teasing, with her pink, hard nipples. I knew all about her real life, because she'd confided in me late at night, after we made love. I knew about the exotic locales in which she'd lived, and about her divorced, ill-suited parents—her Colombian, *macho* millionaire father; her Bronx Jewish socialist mother — the hard times, and the many star-crossed love affairs. If only she would write it straight, I thought, without fancy language, pretentious parrots, and sexy pistachio nuts, people would love it, and she'd be able to sell her books for big bucks and appear on talk shows like Margot Madd, and win prestigious awards like Bill Smith. "What I mean is," I tried not to let my impatience show, "you should write about the night that you lost your virginity to the bearded peasant who worked on your father's plantation, and about how your father disowned you when he discovered the two of you beneath his banana tree. And about how you accompanied your mother on political demonstrations when you were so small that your little arms ached as you held onto the picket signs she made you carry, and how you marched alongside her with tears in your eyes, wishing she would love you, her only daughter, as much as she loved the masses, the downtrodden of the earth. Really, Juanita, it's highly marketable stuff."

To please me, she bought Margot Madd's novel. "I'm studying *At Play* for you, *querido,*" she announced, covering my face with kisses.

One night, however, when she was out, I peeked at the notes she'd scrawled in the book's margin. "This one's a bimbo," she had written, *"una loca!"*

I had another idea. "Call Bill Smith," I told her. "Ask him to come out with us for a drink. And listen to what he has to say about writing. He's a great man. Okay?"

"Okay," she nodded, without enthusiasm.

Bill Smith suggested a bar on Eighth Avenue. It smelled of cheap wine, urine, and cabbage soup. "Great place, isn't it?" he greeted us expansively, stroking his bushy, crumb-laden beard. "A bar for real people, not quiche eaters."

Juanita was the only woman in the place. She was wearing a black catsuit and high heels. The men who lined the bar couldn't take their eyes off her.

We sat at a table in the back. Bill Smith quickly got drunk, and began reminiscing about the alcoholic binges and fistfights of his youth.

Juanita studied her fingernails. Stifling a yawn, she stirred the ice in her Cuba Libre. Finally, she looked up at him. "I must ask you one thing, Mr. Smith. Don't you ever get bored, just telling it like it is?"

He, like all the other men at the bar, kept staring at her full breasts. "Call me Bill, Juanita," he said thickly. "Nope. How else can you tell it?"

"Oh," she said, throwing back her shoulders proudly, so that her breasts appeared even larger and fuller, "you can tell it as it *should* be. Or as it *could* be. Or as it *would* be if one thing—one particle of dust, one atom, one alpha ray—just one tiny thing in the universe suddenly shifted."

Bill Smith rolled his eyes. I tried to show him, by rolling mine, too, that even though I was her lover, I shared his sympathies.

"Or," Juanita went on determinedly, ignoring our rolling eyes, "one can show it as one fears it, dreads it; one can expose the dark side of *what is*. . . ."

I called for the check.

"Damn," Bill Smith said, opening his wallet, "I left the house without any cash. Would you mind?"

"Yeah, right, I'll just bet you did," Juanita said, scowling and suddenly sounding very Bronx. Nevertheless, she paid.

Bill Smith pinched her butt on the way out of the bar.

She gave him an icy stare and walked haughtily ahead of us to the bus stop.

"I like a girl with spunk," he whispered admiringly to me, "and big bazooms."

"You alienated Bill Smith," I said angrily to her when we got back to my airy, high-ceilinged, one-bedroom apartment, where we'd been spending more and more time. I'd grown tired of her tiny, dark excuse of a home.

"I'm sorry, my darling, but he's such a *bobo*. . . ." Still, she seemed genuinely upset to have displeased me. She walked over to my desk. "Okay, I'll do it!" she cried passionately. "I'll write my memoirs—the *real thing!* Not merely a thinly disguised novel, like your idols Margot Madd and Bill Smith. And," her features grew strangely grim, "you shall be the executor of them when I die."

I went to her and held her tightly. "Don't talk of death," I said. "Talk of rebirth, talk of huge sales and megabucks. . . ."

After that, Juanita sat at my desk every day, every night, writing her memoirs. She frowned and sweated, cursing in both Spanish and English as she labored. I stopped making love to her. I didn't want to sap her energy. After a month, I asked her to read me what she'd written. "My father, the rich, cruel banana baron, was an alcoholic," she began.

"Go on, that's terrific," I said.

She read me the next sentence. "He was also a monkey."

My heart sank. Juanita had written, instead of the first chapter of her memoirs, a surrealistic tale about a family that's half human, half monkey.

I was enraged. She was deliberately tormenting me. She had led me on and mocked me. I no longer loved her. In fact, I hated everything about her: her large, bulbous breasts, her Amazonian height, her Spanish-Bronx accent. I raised my hand to strike her.

She drew back, looking pale and fearful. "Please," she cried, placing her hand over her left breast, "my heart!"

My hand remained poised in the air, ready to strike. "There's nothing wrong with your heart," I said, in a mean and surly tone that matched my mood, "other than that you're cold-hearted, not to give me the one thing—the *only* thing—I ask of you!"

She lowered her eyes. Tears ran down her cheeks. "I tried to write my memoirs, I really did," she said, "but it just wasn't any damned fun, *muchacho.* And," her sobs grew louder, "I've hidden something from you, my darling. I didn't want to alarm you . . . but my heart . . . it really is weak." Eyes still downcast, she proceeded to tell me of the rheumatic fever she'd had as a child, and of the doctors who continually warned her that too much excitement in any form would kill her.

I couldn't say a word, I was too amazed by Juanita's revelations. I allowed my hand to fall by my side.

"You didn't mean what you said before, did you?" she asked, raising her bloodshot eyes to meet mine, "about my being coldhearted? You weren't really going to hit me, were you?"

I waited a long moment. She seemed a stranger to me, a surrealist writer with large breasts, a tear-stained, red face, and an inadequate heart. "I love you more than ever, Juanita," I spoke slowly. "You are even more precious to me now that I know about your heart. I will never, never hurt you. Come here." I was acutely conscious, at that moment, of my long eyelashes, my fine, blond hair, my cheeks as red as a girl's, my very strong, very young heart beating loudly against my very strong, very young chest. I rubbed my hands against her nipples until she moaned. I lifted her blouse and stuck my hands down the front of her tight black stirrup pants and inside her pink nylon panties.

In the months following, I made love to her constantly. Our lovemaking grew wilder, more intense. Her orgasms were tidal waves, earthquakes, tornadoes of passion. I rarely came myself, but that only inflamed me more. I was perpetually erect, an animal in heat, a howling beast, never satisfied. Juanita and I didn't eat, didn't sleep. All we did was make love. Until the night her heart gave out. She died in my arms, in the midst of an orgasm so violent the paintings on my walls shook.

Gently, I eased her off my body. I checked her pulse just to be sure. I shut her eyelids tight, and planted a farewell kiss on those pale, full lips. I had every reason to feel proud of myself, and I did. Here I was, only twenty-two, and I had just committed the perfect murder.

At Juanita's funeral, her skinny, gray-haired mother eyed me suspiciously, but I let my hair fall into my eyes. That way, she couldn't really see me, and by the time I pushed the hair away, she was walking out the door of the funeral parlor, her back erect, no longer conscious of me at all.

Shortly after the funeral, I began writing Juanita's memoirs. It was easy work. I remembered everything she'd told me. I finished the memoirs in six months, ending them at the point where Juanita reads my story, *One Night at a Bar in Philly*, and tells me that I'm destined to become one of the world's greatest writers, and declares her love for me on the spot. I conveniently "discovered" her memoirs in a trunk hidden beneath her bed, and a publisher bought them for a decent sum of money. But they sold poorly and went out of print almost overnight.

A year later, a famous literary critic at Yale published a book about Juanita — *Bronx Surrealist* — which won a Pulitzer. All of Juanita's novels were reprinted with brightly-colored drawings of parrots and womens' breasts on the covers. Juanita's work had entered the canon. Suddenly, everyone was teaching her, from the deconstructionists to the feminists, the elitists to the populists. Juanita's books were selling like hotcakes. Her mother, the executor of her daughter's fiction, grew rich and started a progressive magazine with her money, called *The Old Left Writes!*

All Juanita had made me executor of was the book she'd never written, the book I'd written for her, the book which was viewed as her one weak effort and not reprinted. "Not up to snuff," Bill Smith had written in his review in the *Times*. "Appel's memoirs are too down-to-earth, too *real* for her. Unlike those of us who write best of what we know — drinking and fighting, for instance — Juanita's true calling was to write about the exotic universes of her imagination."

So these days I lie in bed, sweating, staring at the ceiling, unable to sleep, trying to understand what happened. And what I think is this: Juanita had been aware of my murderous intentions all along; Juanita had been in control every step of the way. After all, she's the one who told me about her weak heart and the doctors' warnings. And then I think that I don't even exist at all, that Juanita had simply conjured me up — so very young, hungry, pretty, and greedy — to help her achieve her wild and glorious climax, the ending she'd undoubtedly yearned for. But most of all, as I lie here, night after night, never sleeping, I fear that soon I shall be forced to create my own climax, my own ending. Because I see now that a life without Juanita is really no life at all.

★ ★ ★

Cruise Control

VINCENT DESTEPHANO, WEARING
his lightweight khaki suit, sitting alone at a table in a
hotel bar on West Fifty-seventh Street and staring at a redheaded woman wearing a sleeveless black dress, had a revela-
tion: *his was a life on cruise control.* He'd never thought about
it quite that way before, but it was true. In Charlottesville,
where he now lived, it was easy to take the smooth and
steady course, with no bumps on the road, no sharp and
unexpected curves. He loved Charlottesville, its comfort,
architecture, history, and privilege. Privilege, especially, struck
Vincent as a beautiful thing.

Pouring himself a second glass of white wine and staring
at the woman, who was sitting a couple of tables over, and
whose bright red hair shone even in the dimly-lit hotel bar,
he wondered for the first time whether it would be good for

his children to grow up taking such privilege for granted, or whether they would become weak and spoiled. He'd wanted them to go to good schools, to live without fear and violence. Most of all, though, he wanted them to belong somewhere. As a boy, growing up on the streets of the Bronx, he had never felt that he belonged.

But he'd found a way out: working two part-time jobs, he'd put himself through law school in Baltimore. Now he worked for a small firm in Charlottesville, which, as far as he was concerned, was another planet from the Bronx, located in another galaxy. He had a sweet, blond, blue-eyed wife named Katie. They had two children: James, who looked like Katie, and Lisa, who looked like Vincent, with dark eyes and hair, olive skin, and strong features. Sometimes Vincent watched Lisa as she played with her blond girlfriends, and she stood out, like a gypsy child.

Vincent was trim and muscular. As a boy, he'd played stickball on the streets. Now he played tennis three mornings a week. He liked the discipline of tennis; he liked anything that made him feel in control. His parents had prided themselves on being out of control, on being volatile and hot-tempered. Every night during dinner in their cramped, dark apartment on Gun Hill Road, there were curses and arguments, and sometimes the shattering of plates and glasses. His two sisters, Anna-Maria and just plain Maria, frequently fled the table in tears, their meals half-eaten, their black mascara running down their faces. Sometimes, after dinner, his father would take the strap to him. His friends in Charlottesville frequently asked him questions about his Bronx childhood; it was such a curiosity to them. He romanticized it, making it sound palatable and familiar, a situation comedy on TV: the larger-than-life Italian mama and papa with their hearts of gold, always eating spaghetti and chicken cacciatore.

Pouring himself a third glass of wine, he watched the red-headed woman, who was now reapplying her red lipstick, which was even brighter than her hair. He promised himself that this would be his final glass. But, being back in New York, even for two days, depressed him, and the wine made him feel better. His widowed mother, old and sick and super-stitious, wanted, at last, to return to her people in Sicily. He had been called in to help. He'd spent the last two days going through stacks of papers, trying to remain calm, even when his mother went on and on about how the ghost of his father came to her every night, mad as hell at all of them, but espe-cially at Vincent, who had moved far away from the family, who had deserted and betrayed them all.

The redheaded woman was raising her arms over her head, stretching. Her movements were feline, full of confidence. She was the only woman at a table full of men. He recognized her, in a way, although he'd never seen her before. She was one of them, one of "the girls," as he called them. As a teenager, he'd been drawn to them, to that type: the lone female in the group of guys, the one girl the boys felt so at ease with, they drank and bowled and played cards with her. The girl was always pretty, slightly rowdy, very smart, and sensual beyond her years. Not indiscrimately sensual, of course. The girl was never the tramp.

Anna-Maria, his younger sister, was not one of the girls. She had married Louis Colucci from the Gun Hill Projects. They had three kids, and they still lived in the Bronx, on Arthur Avenue. They'd wanted Vincent to stay overnight with them. But it had been on Arthur Avenue that he'd been beaten up one hot summer night by a gang of boys from a rival high school, and it was there, the next night, that he'd returned with his own friends from Gun Hill Road for ven-gence, armed with baseball bats and switchblades. No, he didn't want to spend an evening on Arthur Avenue.

His older sister, just plain Maria, had also never been one of the girls. Maria had been less fortunate than Anna-Maria. Mickey Piscatello had gotten her pregnant while she was still in high school. Mickey had gone on to become a big-time drug dealer in Las Vegas, abandoning her in the process. She'd raised her child alone, in a one-bedroom apartment in Yonkers, on a secretary's salary. She had no extra room for Vincent. So he was staying, instead, in this snazzy hotel near Carnegie Hall, with its dimly-lit hotel bar, where the waiters all affected British accents and glided swiftly along, almost as though dancing, and where, no matter how hard he tried, he just couldn't stop staring at the redheaded woman.

After he'd started college, and had begun separating from his family and the streets, he'd given up the girls. The girls were too restless, too flirtatious and quick-witted, too passionate and demanding. In order to become the kind of man he so much wanted to be, he'd had no choice but to give them up.

And he hadn't really minded. He never thought about them one way or another, after he'd met Katie. Katie, born and bred in Charlottesville, had never gone barhopping with the guys, had never sat out on a stoop drinking beer, smoking and cursing and flirting. She'd gone to Sweet Briar, had majored in Home Economics, ridden horses, been in a sorority, and dated fraternity boys. Her single act of rebellion had been marrying an Italian guy from the Bronx. But Vincent made it clear to Katie's parents right from the start how much he hungered to enter their world, how much more he valued their world than his own, and they soon accepted him. Really, Katie barely understood how different his background was from her own. Not that she was stupid. She was, however, sheltered, and her imagination couldn't include that which she didn't know existed. Besides, he didn't talk much about his past, about Gun Hill Road, about violent fights with baseball bats, about sniffing glue from paper bags in parking lots late at night, about having a father who cursed at you and then took a strap to you when you weren't even sure what terrible crime — or, perhaps, what mortal sin — you had committed. The few times Katie had met his parents and his sisters, she'd just been bewildered.

But this redheaded woman in the hotel bar, sitting with all the men, laughing so loudly, so flirtatiously, well, it annoyed him that he couldn't stop watching her. She was probably in her early thirties, not really a girl at all. She wore her sleek, shiny hair in a geometric bob, like a twenties' film star. Her jewelry was all silver: a large necklace in the shape of an elephant; long, dangling earrings; and serpentlike bracelets coiled along each of her bare upper arms.

He had never been unfaithful to Katie. Lots of his friends in Charlottesville fooled around while their wives looked the other way. But he didn't want to. First, there was the issue of morality. All those confessions at the Immaculate Conception Church, across the street from the projects, had left their mark. Second, none of the women he met down in Charlottesville had ever tempted him much. There was nothing they could offer him that Katie didn't already provide.

The redheaded woman took a long sip of her drink. Briefly, she rested her head on the shoulder of one of the men, a man with a blond beard and a turtleneck sweater. She definitely wasn't on cruise control. She and the men ordered another round of drinks and laughed some more. He felt stodgy and stale in his southern-gentleman khaki suit, with his dark, wavy hair so neatly combed.

The waiter appeared. "Sir?" he asked Vincent politely, in his quasi-British accent, lifting the empty wine bottle from the table. Despite himself, Vincent ordered a second bottle.

He glanced at his watch; it was late, midnight, and the girl's party appeared to be breaking up. One by one, the men rose and kissed her good-bye. She remained at the table, alone. A moment later, she stood up and walked over to him. "You've been watching me all night," she said. Her voice was soft, but she spoke boldly and directly, which was the way the girls always spoke, he remembered.

"Yes," he said. He'd been wrong in thinking that she hadn't noticed him. He felt all the excitement, all the unruly and pent-up energy, of a teenage boy.

She sat down next to him. He offered her a glass of wine, but she shook her head. She called the waiter over. "A Campari and soda," she said. She turned back to Vincent. "Why?" she asked him.

"Why?" he repeated her question, not understanding. Her eyes were an intense, bright blue.

"Why have you been watching me all night?"

"You're so pretty." He surprised himself by his boyish candor. "Also, you remind me of girls in my past."

"But not in your present?"

"No. Not in my present." He let the statement hang there. She could interpret it however she wanted—that he yearned to have someone like her in his life, or the opposite. He wasn't sure which he preferred. "Why did you come over to me?" he asked. "Because you were watching me." She made it sound as though it were the most obvious thing in the world. She sipped her Campari and soda.

"The way you look," he pointed to her exotic bracelets, suppressing an urge to reach out and stroke the bare, pale, slightly freckled skin of her arms, "you must be used to being watched." He did one of those clichéd male numbers — gazing at her body suggestively — and immediately felt embarrassed. But she didn't seem to notice, or care.

She nodded. "Well, I didn't come over just because you were watching me. It's also because I don't want to be alone. All of my friends were going home, and I didn't want to go back to my apartment. Also, *you* sort of remind me of someone in my past, too."

He felt even more embarrassed, so he changed the subject. "What was the occasion for your get-together with your friends?"

"It was a celebration for Joey Gardner, the playwright, maybe you know, he had a play off-Broadway a few years ago, *Moving Forward*?"

Vincent shrugged, and smoothed the sleeve of his neatly-pressed jacket. Of course, he didn't know.

"Anyway," she went on, not seeming to mind at all that he'd never heard of her friend, "Joey just got a big grant. First time ever. I can't tell you how many times he's applied for Guggenheims and NEAs, for instance. and the group of us who were out tonight, we all met a few years ago at an artists' colony upstate, and we keep up with each other, celebrate each other's successes, you know."

"Why didn't you want to go home?" he asked. He felt strangely comfortable asking her such a personal question.

She frowned. "I just broke up with the man I've been living with for eight years. It was my choice, but even so. . . ." She looked into her glass.

"Are you a playwright, too?"

"No. I'm a poet."

Some of Katie's girlfriends had recently formed a poetry-writing group. Katie had been thinking of joining, too. By next year they'd be bored of poetry, and they would discover pottery or quilting. He didn't fault them for it. But he did sense that this woman was the real thing. Even though, with her black dress and exotic jewelry, she could just as well have been some bohemian dilettante, but he knew she wasn't. He continued to feel like a teenager around her: intimidated, nervous, and yet, very bold and very aroused, all at the same time.

"Where did you grow up?" he asked, trying to place her. Maybe if she told him about her background, she'd seem less magical, less arousing, less threatening.

"Brooklyn," she answered, as though eager to help him out in his quest to demystify her. "Sheepshead Bay. There's nothing at all poetic about my past." She smiled, and her teeth were slightly crooked. "I started publishing my poems in very little magazines right after I graduated from college. I *still* publish my poems in very little magazines." She laughed. "But I've also got three books out, with good presses."

He could place her now. In high school, she'd been the editor of the literary magazine. She'd dressed all in black back then, too. She'd definitely been "the girl" in her crowd, the one who'd hung around with the hip boys, the boys who also wrote poetry. He'd been aware of those girls, of course, but he had his own crowd, his own girls. In his crowd, nobody wrote poetry.

"Where did you grow up?" she asked.

Maybe she was as drawn to him as he was to her. Maybe she was also hoping to demystify him. He didn't hesitate. "The northeast Bronx. Gun Hill Road."

"Gun Hill Road," she repeated, making the three words sound almost musical. "I have a friend who grew up on Gun Hill Road. Lucy Zucchino," she said.

He stared at her. He had been friendly with Lucy's older brother, Petey Zucchino. Petey had been one of the few other guys from the neighborhood, who, like Vincent, had managed to earn high grades, and yet somehow also to pass muster with the tough boys. Vincent remembered little Lucy, too, a cute kid with braces and early-budding breasts.

"Lucy and I met at my health club," the woman went on. "We swim together three mornings a week. She's a photographer for a New Jersey newspaper, and she lives uptown, near Columbia." She tapped her glass with a long red fingernail and looked thoughtful. "You know, she *has* mentioned her older brother to me. He lives out in L.A. I think he's a film editor."

Suddenly, Vincent very much wanted to see them—Lucy and Petey Zucchino, who'd both survived those mean streets, unlike so many of the others. Billy Reticliano had become a junkie. Joey DeCroco had died in Vietnam. Rosemary Rizotta, who'd once been so lively and pretty, still lived with her parents on White Plains Road, afraid to go out by herself ever since she'd been brutally raped by a gang of boys in Bronx Park on the evening of her twentieth birthday. It made his heart soar just to think about Lucy and Petey. He wanted to throw his arms around them and say, "We are the survivors! The pioneers!" He knew it was a crazy, drunken thought, but, nevertheless, he felt love at that moment for Lucy and Petey Zucchino.

He also felt something akin to love for this redheaded woman, this bearer of such good news about Lucy and Petey. He wanted to throw his arms around her, too, to hug her tightly to his chest. Instead, he held tightly onto his wine glass, and began telling her all about how he used to hang around with Petey Zucchino in the old days. He told her about how, when he and Petey had been about twelve, they'd been caught trying to steal cigarettes from old Mr. Riccio who ran the corner candy store, and how Mr. Riccio had gotten them to sweep the floor for free in the store for a month after that by threatening to tell the cops on them. Then he found himself telling her about his superstitious, Old-World mother in her black dresses and stockings, and her insistence that the ghost of his father came and cursed him out every night. He told her about his father and the strap. And about Anna-Maria and just plain Maria. About Katie and his two kids, and how he lived on cruise control in beautiful, historic Charlottesville, Virginia, home of Thomas Jefferson and Monticello. And about "the girls," and how he'd always been drawn to them.

She sat quietly, her elbows on the table, sipping her second Campari and soda. Her expression was serious. When she finally leaned back and spoke, her voice was soft. But again, she was direct. "Do you like living on cruise control?"

"What about you," he asked, instead of answering, "do you like *your* life?"

She didn't hesitate. "Well, I like writing poetry. Even though there's no money and no glory in it. I mean, nobody reads poetry any more, right?"

He certainly couldn't remember the last time he'd read a poem. But he didn't say anything, and she didn't seem to expect him to.

"Of course, some poetry," she went on, "can lead you to a certain respectability, to a tenured academic post some-where. But my poems are more raw and sexual — more wicked."

"The girls," he said, "are always wicked. It comes with the territory."

She went on. "But the man I just broke up with, well, in the end I didn't like him very much. Or who I was when I was around him. He's a lot older than I am. He's a poet, too. But the last few years, he wanted me to stop writing. He'd become too respectable, a man of letters, a big-shot acad-emic. My work began to embarrass him."

He wanted to lean over and kiss her, to tell her that *he* would never, never ask her to stop writing, that he would die for her right to create sexy, raw poems. It was time to go, he thought. Time to say that it had been a pleasure to meet her, time to wish her good luck with her poetry and her love life, and then to depart. He paused, and said, "Would you like to come upstairs to my room with me?"

"No."

The wind went out of him, as though she'd punched him, hard, in the stomach. On the other hand, he felt relieved, too. She was making it easy for him. There was no temptation. She didn't even *want* to go to bed with him. She'd just been chatting with him, making idle talk, killing time. His revelations about his life had meant nothing to her. She traveled in circles where people revealed themselves all the time. In New York City, total strangers shared their life stories on the subway each morning. Her lack of interest in him was liberating; he could keep on living on cruise control.

"I'd rather you came back with me, to my apartment," she said.

He laughed aloud with the pleasure of it all, with the roller-coaster—like emotions she was bringing out in him. He felt exhilarated. He felt boyish. He felt terrified. What if Katie called him at the hotel in the middle of the night? What if there were an emergency at home? He had no answer. All he knew was that he was going home with her, with "the girl," a redheaded, blue-eyed poet from Sheepshead Bay who swam three mornings a week with Lucy Zucchino from Gun Hill Road.

"My name is Barbara," she said, as they stood outside the hotel and hailed a taxi together. "Barbara Stock."

"Vinny," he said, helping her into the taxi. "Vinny De-Stephano." It had been a long time since he'd referred to himself as Vinny, instead of Vincent.

Her apartment was in Chelsea, on the top floor of a small building wedged between a twenty-four-hour greengrocer and a Mexican restaurant. He followed closely behind her, up the five long flights of stairs, wondering if she could feel his breath upon her neck.

She led him into her living room. He looked around, surprised that the room appeared so cold and inhospitable. Nobody he knew in Charlottesville decorated their homes like this, with geometric, sharply-angled steel and black furniture. It was "postmodern," he decided — a word he'd read in magazines — but then he decided that, after all, he liked those sharp angles, those edges and hard lines, precisely *because* nobody else he knew would like it.

"Something to drink?" she asked. "All I have is a can of Pepsi and a can of ginger ale."

"Ginger ale," he said, sitting down uncomfortably in one of the chairs.

She went off to the kitchen, and he tried to adjust his body to the angular chair. One of her books was lying out on the square steel coffee table: *Spectrum: Poems by Barbara Stock*. It was a slim volume. The cover illustration was of a bright red cloud floating in a turquoise sky. He turned the book over. In the author's photograph on the back, she looked even more like a twenties' film star than she did in person; her lips were poutier, her eyes more luminous. Above the photo, there was a quote. "Barbara Stock's poems," he read, "do what all good poems must do — they force you to question your vision of the world." He opened the book. "For Al," he read, "who has taught me so much about the ambiguity of poetry. And also in memory of Rick, who taught me so much about the ambiguity of life."

Al, Vincent guessed, was the older poet. He felt irrationally jealous and resentful of Al. He felt a tough boy's urge to fight Al, to take him out on Arthur Avenue in order to establish his claim on Barbara Stock. As for Rick, whomever he was, he was dead, so there was no reason to take him out. He closed the book. He didn't feel ready to read any of her poems.

She returned with the two sodas. She'd stuck a curved plastic straw — a child's straw — into each can. He felt more boyish than ever as he sipped his soda through the straw. When she inserted the straw between her own red lips, however, it struck him as anything but childish. It was so erotic, so arousing, that he had to look away. "Listen," he said, not looking at her, "you said, back at the hotel, that I reminded you of someone in your past."

She was sitting across from him in a chrome chair identical to his, although she seemed comfortable in hers. She spoke so softly he had to lean forward to hear. "That's right."

"Who?" he pressed. "Who do I remind you of?"

She looked up. "You remind me of my first love," she said. "Of my one great love."

He was struck by her language. *Her one great love* . . . he'd never known anyone who spoke like that, or at least, who spoke like that and sounded genuine.

"In high school," she went on, slowly, "I was the editor of the literary magazine. It was called *the Ladder.* I hung around with the other kids on the magazine staff, the kids who wrote poetry and short stories, you know the type."

He refrained from smiling with the knowledge of how right he'd been in his assessment of her. He simply nodded.

"I had boyfriends. Boys who quoted Camus and Kerouac. To use your expression, I was one of the girls. I smoked pot with the guys, went to museums and foreign films and hung out in the Village with them, all that. But there was always something missing for me. There . . . was this boy. I would see him in the hallway. I would see him in the cafeteria, sometimes hanging around with his friends outside the school. He was tough, Italian, he hung out with the bad crowd, the boys who were always in and out of trouble, who ended up expelled from school. Boys who did hard drugs, robbed liquor stores . . . well, *you* know."

Again, he nodded. He knew.

"He and I were absolutely worlds apart." She sighed. "Listen, this part of my life, when I try to tell it to anyone now, it just sounds like a grade-B movie. Are you sure you want to hear?"

He nodded, watching her as she sipped her Pepsi and crossed her legs and slipped off her black shoes, which, to Vincent, looked like the delicate slippers a ballerina would wear.

"Well, I kept noticing this boy. He and I would exchange glances. I would flush when I saw him. . . . I never told anyone about him. This went on for *two years,* you have to understand, all through tenth and eleventh grade. Two years is a really long time when you're a kid. Finally, early in the fall of my senior year I couldn't stand it any more. I walked right up to him. It was three o'clock, and he was standing in front of the school, lighting up a cigarette. 'Why are you watching me?' I asked him."

"That's the same thing you asked me," Vincent said, surprised.

She nodded. "Yes. The same thing. And he answered just the way you did, too. He said, 'Because you're so pretty.' And then he said, 'Let's talk.' I just couldn't believe it. This bad boy wanted to *talk* to me. I brought him home with me. Both of my parents worked. His name was Rick Giampino. He was one of seven kids. His father was an unemployed gambler. His mother drank. I read him my poems, and he listened so seriously, more seriously than any other boy had listened to me before, and we made love. I mean, we were seventeen, and we made love that very day, all afternoon. And after that we saw each other as often as we could. But we hid our involvement. We knew that everyone — his family and friends, my family and friends, our teachers, everyone — would try to break us up. And of course the tension of having to hide our relationship added a fierce eroticism to things. . . . And then I got pregnant." She paused, sipped her Pepsi through the straw. Her voice grew even softer. "I was on the pill, but I'd grown careless. When I found out I was pregnant, I fell apart. I didn't tell my parents, or my friends. I didn't tell Rick, either. I just refused to see him, and I wouldn't tell him why. It drove him crazy. I totally rejected him."

"Why?" Vincent asked. She seemed to be leaving something out.

"I don't know," she said, without expression. "I've asked myself that question every single day for years. Why? I've asked therapists. I've asked my friends. I used to ask Al, the man I lived with. He said it was because I had gotten myself into a situation I couldn't control and unconsciously I wanted out of it. But I don't know. I just don't know."

Vincent was silent. He was surprised that poets — people who spent their entire lives exploring feelings — didn't always know why they did the things they did.

"I carried very small," she went on, "and my mother didn't figure it out until I was in my sixth month. I was sent away. I had a girl. I gave her up for adoption. Sometimes I dream about her, that she's all grown up and that she looks exactly like Rick. When I returned home, Rick had another girl-friend, a girl from his crowd, a girl with a drug problem. I heard that he'd also gotten into drugs. A year later, he over-dosed and died. For years, I felt responsible for his death. Sometimes I still feel that way. Al hated it when I used to say that. Sometimes I fantasize that Rick is alive, that he didn't die, that he kicked drugs and that he lives a quiet and simple life on cruise control some place far away, like Charlottesville, Virginia. And that I'll run into him one day in a hotel bar on West Fifty-seventh Street, or someplace equally far-fetched."

He rose from the chair. He kneeled down in front of her and he ran his fingers through her sleek red hair.

She sat very still. "To tell you the truth, I'm terrified right now."

"Of me?" He continued to stroke her hair.

"Yes. I mean, you're not Rick. What you are is a complete stranger. And I've let you into my home. You could be a murderer, a . . ."

"I'm not," he said. He kissed her.

She kissed him back without any hesitation at all. She placed her thin, pale arms on his shoulders.

They kissed for a long time, and then he followed her into her bedroom. He watched her undress. Her pale, narrow-waisted body was unbearably beautiful. Standing there, watching her, he understood why they had come to be together, why they were going to make love. In each other's arms, they were both seeking forgiveness and absolution for past sins — the real sins, and the imagined ones. He hoped that after they made love they didn't feel even more like sinners than before. He began unbuttoning his shirt. No matter where it led him, though, he was going to do it, he was going to follow this dangerous and unexpected curve in the road.

★ ★ ★

Nautilus

CLAUDIA WAS IN LOVE — DEEPLY, passionately in love — with the Leg Press machine at her health club. She liked the other Nautilus machines just fine: the Pulldown was kind of cute; the Leg Extension had a certain macho charm. But it was the Leg Press she loved. She knew, of course, that it wasn't "rational" to love a machine; she also knew, however, that the truest romantic love, the kind of love about which the great poets throughout the centuries had written, was never rational. So she wasn't worried about herself; rather, she felt blessed to be in such a rapturous, joyous, sensual state.

It had been love at first sight, from her very first tour of the Upper East Side health club with Nanci, the snooty membership director, who'd kept looking at Claudia's discount store, nondesigner clothes with disdain. The club was really much too expensive for Claudia. She had come just out of curiosity, to see what a high-class health club looked like. She'd always belonged to rundown YMCAs in the past. So this time she'd decided to treat herself to something with a little more style than a Y, although certainly not a club like this one, which she'd heard was the second or third most expensive in the city.

Besides, the main thing—all that she really wanted to do for her body — was to trim down from a size six to a size four. Almost any club with a single treadmill would do. She didn't need a fern bar, a restaurant, and a lounge with plush sofas and TV sets. But none of that mattered. Because once Claudia saw the Leg Press out of the corner of her eye, as Nanci walked her around the Nautilus floor, Claudia knew her destiny. Immediately, heart pounding, face flushed, Claudia had informed Nanci — who appeared stunned by Claudia's eagerness—that she didn't need to see any more of the club, not the pool, not the sundeck, not the sauna. She was ready to sign.

Nanci took out all the necessary papers, although she remained tight-lipped and unsmiling as Claudia signed on the dotted line. Nanci probably expected her check to bounce, Claudia realized. But Claudia didn't care what Nanci thought. Nanci couldn't possibly know that she had just fallen in love, and that one of Claudia's deepest-held beliefs was that money— or one's lack of it— must never interfere with love; she was sure that some great poet, somewhere, sometime, had written that.

Back when Claudia had been in love with Juan, the compulsive gambler who'd kept lying to her about how he no longer gambled, he'd literally abandoned her one night while they stood waiting in line for a movie. "Vegas," he mumbled to her, his eyes wild, "I gotta." And suddenly, sweating like a pig, he'd raced off the line, hailed a taxi to the airport, and flown to Las Vegas. Claudia — who also believed with all her heart and soul in tracking down lovers who abandon you — immediately booked herself a flight to Vegas, as well, even though she'd been between jobs at the time, and the last thing she could afford was a trip to Vegas. But she had loved Juan.

Unfortunately, by the time she got to Vegas, Juan already had gambled away all he had, and — as she begged him in the hotel lobby to come home with her and to let her help him — he'd shouted at her that she was too clingy and needy, and she should get the hell out of his life once and for all. It wasn't a moment she liked to remember. But Juan was ancient history, she reminded herself, as Nanci escorted her politely, but coolly, out of the health club. The Leg Press was her present, and her future, both. And the most wonderful thing about the Leg Press was that, unlike Juan, it wasn't going anywhere. Not to Vegas. Not to Atlantic City. Not anywhere. Ever.

There did turn out to be a dark side to her new love affair, however. She should have expected it: after all, the great poets always wrote about the dark side as well as the raptures of love. In her case, it was having to share the Leg Press with the other members of the club.

Claudia would watch, every day, as both male and female members sat down inside the Leg Press's cozy seat, wriggled their fannies suggestively in order to get comfortable, adjusted the weights on the machine, and then, worst of all, lifted their legs and pressed the great big block of metal back and forth, back and forth, in a hideous parody of sex. The sight of them repelled Claudia; she grew wildly jealous. She wanted to pull them off the machine — men and women both — and tear them apart, limb by limb. But she couldn't; she didn't want Nanci to rescind her membership.

The very worst were the beautiful women, of course. And there were plenty of them. Women with flowing blond hair, and petite, size-four bodies with suspiciously enormous breasts, who always wore the tiniest of workout bras, and shorts that looked more like panties than workout gear.

Still, Claudia was confident that it was she whom the Leg Press loved. She knew that the Leg Press, when it let those women sit on it and wriggle their fannies, well, it was just the Leg Press's job. It was a gig. It was what the Leg Press had to do to earn its keep. It meant no more to the Leg Press than that.

And Claudia truly empathized with having to earn one's keep. She also understood plenty about jobs that were just meaningless gigs. After college, even with her A+ average as an English major, she just couldn't get excited about doing anything. What thrilling career was open to her? Teaching — blah; publishing — not very secure these days; advertising — too much pressure. So she just kept doing secretarial jobs. And they were no more than gigs: all that typing, faxing, and saying, "Mr. So-And-So is on the line, please hold." Currently, she was on her fourth secretarial job since finishing school. Her third boss was the only one who'd actually fired her, outright. He had called her too "mercurial," looking at her as though he didn't even think she had the brains to know the meaning of the word, since she was just a lowly secretary. But what he had thought of her didn't matter, because she now had a new job as a secretary for some city agency, and it was working out fine, since nobody else there seemed to view their jobs as anything more than gigs, either.

Still, she'd begun to resent even this new, easy city job, because it meant that she had such limited time to spend with the Leg Press. The health club's hours were from 6:30

in the morning to ten at night. Claudia's job, which was all the way downtown on Worth Street, was a nine-to-fiver. And she lived way uptown on the West Side. So she had no time for the health club in the morning, since it took her quite a long time to get to work. And then, after work, it took her a long time to get from her job back uptown to the health club. She'd spent hours and hours studying subway and bus maps, but there were no quicker routes than the one she already used.

Finally, though, breathless and rushed, she always did make it to the club after work, even on the very worst days when the subways stalled or the buses never came. She would hurriedly flash her membership card, and then race inside to the locker room to change.

But even that seemed to take an eternity. She always had to be especially careful not to rip her pantyhose or tear a sleeve on her blazer as she hung them inside her locker. Since she'd joined this club, she had no money—none at all—for new work clothes. Instead, she kept buying new outfits for the health club. She really had to, even though her MasterCard was almost at its limit, and she hadn't even paid last month's bill, but what could she do? She needed to look great, truly great, every single time she went out on the Nautilus floor— for the Leg Press's pleasure, of course. She now owned quite a few sexy black Jogbras with matching, skintight Lycra shorts, as well as low-cut thong leotards that revealed her every curve. She had a spangled leotard; a fringed leotard; one covered with shiny metallic studs; and one with peek-a-boo lace all over the bust. Best of all, though, she had one white leotard that was almost completely sheer, and she wore it with no underwear. That was her very favorite.

By the time Claudia finally got to the Nautilus machines, it was usually six-thirty. Sometimes, when she had to stop and go to the bathroom, it could be as late as six-forty-five. Once, she'd been in a subway delay that had lasted over an hour; that day, she hadn't even *seen* the Leg Press until seven-fifty.

Usually, when Claudia arrived on the floor, there were lots of other people. This was the period that the health club staff called rush hour, when the "postwork" crowd came. So Claudia began slowly. She would do her entire workout, moving from machine to machine. She always left the Leg Press for last. It was glorious that way, building up an intense sexual and romantic tension between the two of them. It seemed to her that she and the Leg Press each grew more and more consumed by desire and passion, as she went around to all the other machines, one by one. Claudia would sit on the Pulldown bench, lifting the bar up and down with her arms, eyeing the Leg Press the whole time, and knowing that it, too, was eyeing her.

If, when Claudia finally did arrive at the Leg Press, someone else was on it, it would drive her crazy. She would try not to reveal her impatience, her rage, but sometimes, if the person was taking too long, doing set after set, she would begin to pace back and forth, muttering under her breath. Eventually, though, her turn always came. And then she would forget about all the others in the room, all the others in the club, all the others in the world. She was in heaven. She would do four sets of twenty-five repetitions at 120 pounds. That was extremely good, she knew, but not good enough. One day she would do more — she would be so strong she would be able to do hundreds and hundreds of sets, without ever stopping, and then nobody else would be able to get near the Leg Press again, because there she'd always be, moving her strong, muscular legs back and forth, back and forth, endlessly.

Around eight o'clock, the club would empty out. The

postwork crowd was finished. They would head off to wherever it was they headed: home to feed their children; out to
bars to meet friends; to the theater; Claudia didn't care, as
long as they were gone. And once they were gone, usually
she and two or three serious bodybuilders were the only
ones left on the floor. The bodybuilders rarely paid any
attention to the Leg Press. They were enormously pumped-
up men, steroid users, Claudia suspected, interested only in
the free weights and "spotting" each other. Even most of the
club staff was gone. Usually, one Nautilus trainer remained
behind, half asleep in a corner somewhere. So finally Claudia
would have a couple of hours alone with the Leg Press, just
enough for some cuddling. She always felt too self-conscious
to go any further than that, with the bodybuilders and the
trainer still on the floor.

Then one day, she had a brilliant idea. She couldn't believe
it hadn't occurred to her earlier. One night soon, she would
hide somewhere — the ladies' room seemed the obvious
choice — and then, after the club had closed for the night,
she would emerge. And she would head straight to the Leg
Press. And then at last, they would be able to spend an entire
night alone together. She would bring an alarm clock with
her, so that she could easily slip back into the ladies' room
before the club opened, and then emerge in her workout
gear, just another early morning user. And she didn't care if
she was late for work that morning; it would be worth it.

She chose a Monday night. She wore the nearly sheer
white leotard. After all her working out she was down to her
desired size four, and her body now boasted some fetching,
tight little muscles, too, so she knew she looked smashing.
Everything went smoothly. She hung around the club, and
after the rush-hour crowd had left, she sauntered into the
ladies' room and locked the door. She waited a half hour, just

to be on the safe side. Finally, with her lipstick and mascara freshly applied and her leotard clinging just so, she sauntered out. The club was empty; everyone was gone. Although the lights were out, her heart would lead her, even in the darkness, to the Leg Press.

And then, it happened: her life became transformed, became poetry, just as she had imagined it during daytime hours, and dreamed it at night. She and the Leg Press were intimate all night, a kind of intimacy she had never before experienced. Juan had been a bad joke, she now realized. The Leg Press knew how to envelop her, how to guide her, to lead her into just the right back-and-forth motion that would give her the ultimate ecstasy she always had yearned for, and which nobody, certainly not Juan, ever had been able to provide.

She and the Leg Press made love for hours — six hours, eight hours, ten, twelve — she lost all sense of time as she pushed and pulled, and it coached and caressed. Her own body was on fire; she also felt the heat emanating from the Leg Press, and for a moment she feared it would ignite into genuine flames. But the moment passed; they were safe, she knew. Their love was so pure and strong, no harm would come to them. She was sweating and moaning, and her sheer leotard now clung to her like a second skin. And how hard and firm the metal of the Leg Press was; she loved its hardness; no mere man could ever be so hard.

When the alarm clock rang, warning her that it was six A.M., she shut it off. To hell with it. Let them find her with the Leg Press. Who cared? Who cared what any of them thought? None of them, she was certain, had ever had an evening like her's. Not Nanci, not the steroid-taking body-builders and the bored Nautilus trainers; not even the anorexic blond bimbos. She began to laugh. She laughed so hard, she was gasping and writhing, all at the same time. Her laughter felt like music to her — like the music of poetry — and she had a fierce desire to dance to her own inner music. She rose to her feet. And gracefully, she danced all around the Leg Press, a stunning, erotic dance of love and gratitude. She continued to laugh all the while.

Two of the staff Nautilus trainers came in a little early. She continued to dance and to laugh. They stared at Claudia with even more disbelief than Nanci had exhibited when Claudia had first signed on as a club member. "Calm down," the Nautilus trainer on the left said to Claudia. Claudia could tell he was trying to sound authoritative and in control of the situation. "Screw you," Claudia said, still dancing her erotic, sensual dance of love, "What do you know?"

The Nautilus trainers began to walk slowly, backwards, up the stairs to the reception area, staring at Claudia the whole time. Claudia kept dancing and laughing. No members came out onto the floor to start their workout routines.

Instead, some men rudely interrupted her dance, and pulled her away from the Leg Press. She kicked one of them — the one pulling on her left arm — hard in his groin with her powerful, muscular leg. He cried out in pain, but still they managed to pull her away, despite his being doubled over the whole time. They took her to the hospital, where she was examined by a group of doctors. She refused to answer any of their questions. But they made diagnoses, anyway.

"Schizophrenia," one doctor said. He looked to Claudia like a baby-faced parody of Freud with his little round glasses, bushy beard, and smelly pipe.

"Erotomania," announced another, a handsome one with the kind of chiseled features Claudia associated only with fake doctors on TV soap operas.

"Bipolar disorder," declared another. He was the most nattily dressed, and Claudia thought he must be a bigshot, because there was a moment of silence before anyone else dared to offer another diagnosis after his.

But then they started again; they couldn't seem to stop themselves. They went round and round: "Borderline," they said; "Hysteria"; "Obsessive-Compulsive Disorder." Nobody agreed; they argued; then they tried to flatter each other; but still, even with all the flattery, nobody agreed.

One of them tried to talk to Claudia again. "Why were you dancing?" he asked, in what Claudia assumed was meant to be a kind, nonthreatening tone. She didn't answer. "Had you spent the entire night inside the athletic facilities?" he tried again. Claudia shrugged.

Then they began to shout out the names of medicines. They seemed to Claudia like contestants on TV quiz shows desperately trying to shout out the correct answer in order to win the grand prize. "Prozac!" "Zoloft!" "Lithium!" and some other drugs that had so many syllables they sounded to Claudia like words from outer space. Let her stupid ex-boss who'd been so proud of himself for using the word "mercurial" when he'd fired her try some of these eight-syllable words on for size, she thought.

Then one doctor, who'd been silent throughout, spoke softly and thoughtfully to the others. "She was dancing up and down, up and down, all around that machine, as though she were acting out — for all the world to see — what goes on inside her tortured soul." Claudia stared at him: This doctor, with his tie knotted all wrong, and his mismatched socks, was definitely the only one in the group who still read poetry, the only one who still wept over his patient's sad tales. Claudia liked him the best, although she had no intention of speaking to him, either.

Claudia noticed, too, that there was one doctor in the room who didn't speak at all. He was much too busy staring at her nipples through her sheer leotard. He couldn't stop, not even for one second. "Erotomania," thought Claudia.

Throughout the morning, through all their obsessive questioning of her, and their compulsive chattering, Claudia found it easy to remain silent, no matter which of her body parts they fixated on, no matter what they said. She felt such pity for all of them: with all their years of schooling and with so many degrees between them, they couldn't even recognize a harmless woman in love when she was sitting right in front of them. But then, she didn't want to waste any more time thinking about the doctors and their problems. They meant nothing to her, nothing at all. She cleared her mind and thought only of her lover, the Leg Press. She knew that it, too, was thinking only of her.

★ ★ ★

Health

YOU'RE OBSESSED WITH IT, SO YOU go for a checkup.

Your doctor says that basically you're in excellent health.

Before you can breathe a sigh of relief, she adds, "However, your irregular pap smear *may* indicate a precancerous condition, your shortness of breath *may* indicate asthma, and your severe reaction to Prozac *may* indicate manic-depression."

She sends you to three more doctors — one for cancer, one for asthma, one for manic-depression — who give you tests and then send you home to await results.

While you wait, you try to figure out how in the world, on a freelancer's salary, with paltry health insurance, you're going to be able to pay all these doctors.

You begin to experience stabbing pains where you're sure your cervix is.

You have palpitations and can't breathe.

You go on a manic shopping spree, from TriBeca through SoHo through both the East and West Villages, maxing out your credit cards in the process. Afterward, you go home and drink a Scotch, feeling morbidly depressed because you have no money left.

The results of the tests come back a week later. The three doctors tell you that basically you're in excellent health. You call your first doctor to tell her the good news. She gently suggests that perhaps you have some stress in your life. "Why don't you see a psychotherapist?" she asks, rhetorically.

You find a psychotherapist whose office is a convenient two blocks from your apartment. You explain to her that while in a stress-induced state of mania, you recently maxed out all your credit cards, and that your freelance income is unstable and your health insurance won't cover psychotherapy and you'll be paying for her services out of your own not-very-deep pockets.

She looks so bored, you figure she's heard it all before and won't adjust her rates no matter what you say, so you give up and try to liven up the session by telling her that your friends describe you as "mercurial," "volatile," and "intense." She continues to look bored.

You leave her office and walk five blocks uptown to your health club for a workout. Your former Nautilus trainer is there. You had to stop training with him because you could no longer afford his fee. He comes over to chat while you're doing squats. You tell him you're not happy with your thighs. He gives you a long lecture about how you're oppressed by society's image of feminine beauty, and how you need to break free of that image in order to become a fully liberated woman. You feel ashamed because he's a staunch political conservative and usually you're the one who lectures *him* about his politically incorrect beliefs. You pull a muscle in your thigh and scream out in pain and feel even more ashamed.

During your next session, your psychotherapist tells you that shame is bad for both your mental and physical health.

You leave her office feeling depressed. Everyone knows (your doctor, your former Nautilus trainer, your psychotherapist, and you, yourself) that you will never be good enough, smart enough, thin enough, rich enough, politically correct enough, mentally or physically healthy enough. And you'll never have enough income or good enough health insurance to help you get better.

You fantasize about moving to Canada because you believe that their health care system is more humane and you will be more readily cured there. You are, however, susceptible to very bad colds, and you fear the Canadian winter too much.

So you stay put in your own country, growing increasingly obsessed with your health, as well as increasingly mercurial, volatile, and intense.

Over the years, you experience more irregular pap smears, more shortness of breath, more bizarre reactions to various prescribed and over-the-counter medications, and more muscle pulls in your thigh.

Eventually your obsession with your health feels as familiar as an old shoe or an old friend. You grow to accept it, even to welcome it. And why shouldn't you? After all, basically you're in excellent health. And you're alive.

★ ★ ★

Barbie Goes to Group Therapy

BARBIE SHIFTED UNCOMFORTABLY in the stiff metal chair in which she was sitting. She smoothed her white linen dress so as not to cause wrinkles. She crossed her ankles, taking care not to scuff her white patent-leather high heels. Barbie had chosen to wear all white tonight, in order to remind the other women in the group that she was special. Not many women, after all, were thin enough and confident enough to look fabulous all in white.

She looked around the bleak, shabby room. Six other women, dressed mostly in drab browns and greys, had shown up for this first session of the women's therapy group. They were seated in a ragged circle, also in stiff metal chairs, although, Barbie noted, none of them were being careful about their posture, the way she was. They were hunched and slouched in various unflattering combinations. Eventually, they'll all have back problems, Barbie thought. She took a deep breath, keeping her back straight and thrusting out her large, yet pert and perfectly pointed breasts. None of the six women were looking at Barbie. They were, however, looking at one another, exchanging warm, friendly glances. Barbie wished she hadn't had to come to an all-women's therapy group. "Can't I go to a group with men?" she'd asked. "No, that's the whole point," her press agent and image consultant both had insisted, "it's got to be women." But Barbie knew that most women didn't like her, and the feeling was mutual. Little girls were different, of course. Barbie liked *them* just fine, the legions of little girls who bought the dolls made in Barbie's own image. But once the little girls grew up and put away their Barbies, she had nothing in common with them. All those little girls, Barbie knew, had once dreamed of growing up and becoming just like her: poised, glamorous, and breathtakingly beautiful. But when they didn't grow up to be any of those things, well, then they relegated their Barbies to trunks and attics and closets, hiding their formerly beloved dolls like shameful secrets. Barbie understood that her very existence shamed most women so much they couldn't even bear to look at her. She looked around the room again — yes, each of these drab women definitely had a Barbie hidden somewhere.

Barbie turned her attention to the group leader, who was sitting in the only comfortable chair in the room: a thick, padded leather armchair. The group leader, who was wearing a gray jumpsuit, cleared her throat. Barbie stared at her suspiciously, feeling what she called her "threat antennae" go up. The group leader was awfully young to be a therapist. She was nothing like the older, maternal woman in orthopedic shoes that Barbie had envisioned. And her short red hair was cut in a "downtown chic" style that was much too angular and masculine for Barbie's taste. Already, Barbie didn't like her and she hadn't yet spoken a word.

As though reading Barbie's mind — not that she'd looked over in Barbie's direction — the group leader began to speak: "Let's go around the room and introduce ourselves to one another, shall we?" Although the group leader spoke in warm, encouraging tones, she had a strong Brooklyn accent and a severe lisp. Spittle flew from her mouth while she spoke.

Barbie's threat antennae relaxed. She had nothing to worry about. This woman was no competition, even with her avant-garde haircut, because no man would ever choose a Brooklyn-born woman with a speech impediment over Barbie. Barbie's own speech was irresistible to men: crisp and accentless, with a lilting, flirtatious upswing at the end of every sentence.

A heavyset, androgynous woman in a shapeless grey shift, sitting directly across the room from Barbie, began to speak. She also was no competition. Barbie's threat antennae remained relaxed. The heavyset woman spoke in a whiny, nasal voice — something about having taken care of her bedridden, elderly mother for years. But her mother had just died, and now at last the woman wanted to live for herself, and she felt that being in a group of supportive women would help her.

Barbie stopped listening. The heavyset woman was depressing. When Barbie's own mother had gotten ill, Barbie had bought her a condo in Florida and paid for a full-time nurse. She prided herself on remembering to call her mother long-distance every few weeks. Barbie noticed that the heavyset woman was looking at everyone else in the room during her droning recitation, except Barbie. Yes, Barbie thought, she's so shamed by my exquisite presence, that she can't even look at me. After all, my blond, shiny hair, my seductive, bright blue, bedroom eyes framed by my lush lashes, my pink lips, my perfect, pert breasts — it's all too much for these women. Sighing with pleasure at the thought of her own perfection, Barbie glanced down at her breasts, which peeked so prettily through the white linen fabric of her dress.

"Thanks so much for sharing your feelings with us," the group leader lisped to the heavyset woman. Reluctantly, Barbie looked up from her own breasts, and back at the group. The other women were all smiling at the heavyset woman. Nobody was looking at Barbie.

The woman sitting to the right of the androgynous woman began to speak. Barbie liked her looks a little better. She appeared shy and deferential, wearing a modest brown tweed suit. She kept her eyes downcast, and spoke softly. Once or twice in her life, years ago, Barbie had gotten slightly friendly with a couple of women — she'd lost touch with them, of course — but this woman reminded her of them. If Barbie liked any women at all, and she wasn't sure she did, but *if* she did, she liked shy, retiring types, attractive enough so that she wasn't embarrassed to be seen in public with them, but never attractive or assertive enough to arouse her ever-vigilant threat antennae.

The shy woman continued to speak softly, almost whispering, about falling in love with cold, cruel men. She was hoping, she said, that with the support of other women, she'd learn to break that pattern. Barbie stopped listening. This shy woman would never be able to find a man even close to her own Ken, that was clear. First of all, there *were* no other men like Ken. He, like herself, was sheer perfection. Barbie knew that all those little girls who had bought Ken dolls to date their Barbies had expected to grow up and marry men just as handsome and perfect as Ken. Instead, they married men with bald spots, paunches, and drinking problems—or worse, they didn't get married at all! — and then they felt more ashamed than ever, and the Ken dolls, like the Barbies, were relegated to trunks and attics and closets. Barbie decided she didn't like this shy woman, after all; she seemed hopeless, really, going on and on about wanting to be more assertive with men, when it was obvious that she never could be.

The group leader thanked the shy woman for sharing her feelings. There also were little murmured thank-you's from the other women. Nobody looked at Barbie.

The group leader continued to go around the room, inviting women to speak. Barbie didn't listen carefully to any of the other women, either. One was a suburban mother type, dressed in a brown jersey pantsuit. She lived in New Jersey, and had problems with an unfaithful husband and an anorexic daughter. Yawn, thought Barbie, the bridge and tunnel set.

Another woman had acne scars. Spare me, thought Barbie, I'm not a plastic surgeon.

The two others seemed interchangeable to Barbie. They both wore long brown dresses. They both wept while they spoke, and they said the same things: they hated their jobs, they hated their mothers, they hated their bodies.

It was Barbie's turn.

"And what brings *you* here, Barbie?" the group leader spit into the air, still not looking directly at Barbie. Barbie heard an edge to the group leader's voice that hadn't been there when she'd invited the other women to speak. She's masking her shame with hostility, Barbie thought, which struck her as very unprofessional for a therapist.

Barbie sat up even straighter in the uncomfortable chair. She held her breasts high, sucked in her diaphragm. She smoothed her already smooth, glistening blond hair. "Oh," she said, "I don't have any problems. I'm Barbie, after all. But my press agent and my image consultant both told me that some little girls these days were finding me too cool and off-putting, that my sales are down because I'm not perceived as knowing how to 'bond,' or something. So they thought I should come here, to learn to bond with other females, to learn to be warmer. I told them that this would all blow over, that the store managers were probably just adding the figures up wrong. After all, math SAT scores these days are just terrible. Little girls love me as much as they ever did! I'm Barbie, after all. But they kept insisting that I come here. And Ken said, 'Well, Barbie, you might as well give it a try.' His press agent and image consultants say his sales are down, too, that little girls and little boys are finding him too stiff, sort of unevolved, so he's going to do some of those 'men's movement' things, hugging trees, wearing loincloths, stuff like that. But after all, nobody ever said Barbie and Ken—but especially me, Barbie, I'm the one who started it all!—had to know how to bond. I mean, give me a break. I'm beyond all that."

Barbie waited for the group leader to thank her for sharing her feelings, the way she had thanked all the rest of them. But the group leader was silent. And Barbie realized that even when she'd been talking — and she'd been absolutely honest and open, just as her press agent and image consultant had told her to be!—the other women still hadn't looked at her. And, like the group leader, none of them were even polite enough to thank her.

"Let's take a short break," the group leader lisped. "Sharing our feelings can be very intense." The women all smiled back at her, murmuring appreciatively.

Cows, Barbie thought. How did those cute little girls, those girls who loved to dress up their Barbie dolls and comb their hair and play wonderful games of "Barbie Goes to the Prom" and "Barbie Wins the Miss America Pageant" and "Barbie and Ken Honeymoon in Las Vegas" — how did those little girls grow up to become these spitting therapists, these heavyset androgynes, these suburban moms in atrocious brown pantsuits, these interchangeable clones without any character or personality?

The women stood and left the room together, chattering among themselves. They were speaking so softly that Barbie couldn't hear what they were saying. It was just as well. Nothing they said could ever be of interest to her. She would go through with this first session of the group, since she was already here, but tomorrow morning, she would tell her press agent and image consultant to forget it, that wild horses couldn't drag her to another session. "I'm Barbie, after all," she would say. "I don't have to do anything I don't want to do." If they argued with her, she would remind them that she could always find another press agent and image consultant.

Barbie decided to find a ladies' room during the break, in order to reapply her makeup. One thing she hated was to be seen with fading lipstick or smudged mascara, even by women like these who didn't know the first thing about correct makeup application.

Holding both her head and her breasts high, Barbie rose from her seat and walked gracefully in her high heels out into the hallway. None of the other women were in sight. The hallway was empty. Barbie felt relieved. A sign for the ladies' room said it was on the floor below. But there was also an OUT OF ORDER sign sloppily pasted on the front of the elevator. To her displeasure, Barbie realized she'd have to use the stairs. She opened the door to the only staircase on the floor. It shut behind her with a thud. The staircase wasn't very well lit, but she would find her way. She was Barbie, after all — graceful and sure-footed, even in dark, narrow staircases, even in white high-heeled shoes.

Suddenly, Barbie felt spittle in her face. Wet, smelly spittle. Before she could wipe it off, or gag, she was surrounded. The group leader and all the other women closed around her in the narrow dark staircase. Barbie tried to step backward, toward the door, but they pressed close around her. She was unable to move. She realized that they had tricked her — the elevator wasn't *really* out of order — and now she was trapped inside this staircase with these terrible creatures.

"Oh, Barbie," the women chanted in unison, their voices merging together in a wild, excited rhythm, "with your perfect, pert breasts, your stupid theme wardrobes, your gaudy Glamour Homes, and your vacuous, dazed eyes, you're nothing but a vain bimbo, a narcissistic bitch! You're not nice and perky, you're not sweet and generous, you're not *any* of the things they told us you were when we were little girls!"

Heart pounding, Barbie silently cursed her threat antennae for failing her. Her threat antennae had always protected her from female competition where men were concerned, but now, when she needed them most, they were useless against this new threat, one Barbie had never run into before — the threat of female violence. She couldn't believe that this was happening to her. She was Barbie, after all!

There was a stranglehold on her neck, and it was difficult to speak. But she had to. "But don't you remember," she gasped, "how much you loved me back then?"

"Of course we remember." They spoke in unison. One of them — the heavyset woman — sneered: "I remember it all, Barbie. I loved you so much. You were my best friend, my older sister, my good mother, my alter ego, my fantasy self. I sure *do* remember!"

"I also remember, Barbie," the shy woman said, no longer sounding so shy. "I remember thinking, *Barbie* would never stutter nervously in public, *Barbie* would never be so shy she would nearly pee in her pants when the teacher called on her. I remember you, Barbie, very very well."

The suburban mother slapped Barbie once, sharply, across her face.

Tears came to Barbie's eyes. Her face stung.

"My daughter," the suburban woman said, angrily, "my daughter who's starving herself to death told me just last week that all she wants in the whole world is to look like Barbie!"

"Yes, precisely," the group leader said seriously, "that's exactly the point of therapy — to break free of the past, to break free of *you,* Barbie. *You're* the real reason we're here in the first place, the *only* reason. We paid off your press agent and your image consultant to tell you to come here. You were duped, suckered, jerked around, Barbie-Doll!"

And that was the next to last thing Barbie heard clearly, before the women — now shrieking one bloodcurdling, ear-splitting, terribly unladylike cry — bonded together to throw her perfect body with its large, yet pert and perfectly pointed breasts down the long, dark flight of stairs.

The *very* last thing Barbie heard, however, as she tumbled down the stairs — before she breathed her very last breath, before her poised, graceful body in its white linen dress lay shattered and twisted and broken at the bottom of the stairs — were the group leader's lisping words: "So, ladies, on to Ken, yes?"

★ ★ ★

Jimmy Dean: My Kind of Guy

JIMMY AND I MET AT THAT REALLY famous artists' colony, the one that's been around for a hundred years. I was there to paint landscapes; Jimmy, to write a play. He announced this at dinner, his first night there. He'd grown tired of film acting, he said. He described scenes he'd been forced to play all wrong in *East of Eden* and *Rebel Without a Cause*, scenes he'd wanted to play tough, but which the director had made him play sensitive, and other scenes he'd wanted to play sensitive, but the director had made him go all steely and *macho*. "I want to be my *own* boss," he said, downing his third glass of red wine, "to write, direct, and star in my own play. And don't worry, it'll be a real work of art," he added, as though any of us at the dinner table that night would have doubted his artistry.

I was the only woman at the table. That was because, out of the twenty or so of us in residence at the artists' colony at the time, there were five gay men there, all of whom had major crushes on Jimmy, and all of whom had made beelines for Jimmy's table. "Jimmy is our idol," they'd informed me, the night before his arrival, "with those soulful eyes, that perky nose, that rebel mouth. We believe that in his *heart,* he's one of us — whether he really is or not." The five of them, plus Jimmy, equaled six, exactly the number of chairs at the dinner table. But there was no way — on Jimmy's first night at the colony — that I was going to sit at one of the other tables, trapped next to Olga, for instance, the photographer known for her pictures of human fingers and toes. After all five of the men and Jimmy were comfortably seated, I squeezed in a seventh chair. I wanted Jimmy. I intended to have him. Not for eternity. Just for my stay at the artists' colony.

All week long, before Jimmy's arrival at the colony, the five men — each of whom I had become good friends with — had argued over which of them Jimmy would sleep with first. "Me first, definitely," insisted Gregory, in a state of near-rapture. "I'll win him over with my music." Gregory, a composer, was smug because his works had been performed by the New York Philharmonic. "No, me first," argued Paul, belligerently. Paul was a poet who wore round, clear-framed eyeglasses that slipped down his nose. "Remember, guys," he added, "I'm the film buff in this crowd. Jimmy and I will *bond.*" They were all wrong, but I never said so aloud. It would be *me* first.

Jimmy Dean was ambivalent, ambiguous, tortured, talented, tormented, gorgeous, and noncommittal, and I always click with those guys right away. We see in each other the same swirling, relentless inner turmoil that devours our souls, the same wild desires that drive us so hard, but that are too huge, too scary, even to name. "We have no skin," a former lover once said to me, "there's nothing between *us* and everything else." I don't know where that former lover is now, of course. I never expected to be with him forever. I never *want* forever—with anyone. I'm not that kind of girl. And none of them are that kind of guy. We know that perfection can't last. But we wouldn't exchange our one perfect moment together for a lifetime of anything less.

And I was right: When Jimmy's eyes met mine across the dinner table his first night at the artists' colony, we clicked, clicked, clicked, like a TV remote control gone wild. He just kept talking, though, like nothing out of the ordinary had happened, regaling us with some dishy anecdote about Natalie Wood, Sal Mineo, a bathtub, and a French poodle. He didn't miss a beat. I could tell that not one of the five men sitting at the table with us had any idea what had just happened. After we'd all finished our beef goulash—the colony chef's special, prepared in honor of Jimmy's arrival—I got up from the table and walked outside into the warm summer air, strolling purposefully through the dark woods back to my studio. All I had to do was wait. I sat in my chair in the center of the studio, staring at my own moody paintings hanging on the walls. Moments later, I heard Jimmy's knock on the door. The artists' colony rules strictly forbade residents from conducting love affairs on the premises, and even rebel-without-a-cause Jimmy followed the rules. So he and I hopped onto his motorcyle and drove into town. We booked ourselves a cozy room in a charming Victorian-style hotel, where, within moments, we ended up naked, entwined, on top of a postcard-pretty, four-poster bed.

And in that bed, all night long, Jimmy said all the right things, the things a girl like me just loves to hear. "I don't know who I am," he whispered, staring into my eyes and stroking my lips. His sultry whisper made me even more desirous. Our lovemaking grew wilder. He clawed my back, drawing blood. He cried out, "I'm in agony. I want *this,* but I want *that,* too. Hold me," he commanded, "tighter, tighter, even tighter, really tight, *hurt* me," he said, flinging himself across the four-poster bed. "No, no, let *me* hurt *you,*" he changed his mind, and then, "No! No, let's not hurt each other, let's just lie here and cuddle like two innocent school-children, okay?" He grew insecure. He sat up. "You like this, don't you?" he asked. "Oh yes," I answered. I grew nervous: "Jimmy, am I a good lover?" "You bet," he sighed. We knew how to drive each other crazy with lust, how to play on each others' fears, how to reassure each other tenderly, over and over, all night long.

After that, we spent every night together for the rest of my stay at the artists' colony. We always went back to the room with the four-poster bed, other than one Saturday night, when, just for kicks, we went to a sleazy motel on the highway. By the time my residency had ended, I'd completed over a dozen landscapes, one of which — the most violent and ambiguous — I gave to Jimmy as a parting gift. Jimmy was scheduled to stay on at the colony for two more weeks. He kissed me at the bus station. "My play is almost finished," he said. I nodded, kissing his fingers in farewell one by one, wishing that Olga, the photographer, was there to capture with her camera my lips on his beautiful fingers.

Sometimes, after lovemaking, Jimmy had told me that his play was about a Brooklyn cabdriver named Antonio who yearns to be a boxer. Other times he'd said it was about a young girl named Antoinette who yearns for the love of a tough guy named Tony who won't give her the time of day. Honestly, it didn't matter to me what Jimmy's play was about, or whether he was even writing a play. It also didn't matter to me that — after I'd left the artists' colony and had returned to my gloomy Manhattan studio, where I began a series of black-on-black urban streetscapes — Jimmy began to spend his nights on the four-poster bed with Gregory and Paul, and even with Olga, on one or two occasions. Jimmy and I hadn't had that kind of relationship: it hadn't been about possession, till death do us part, meeting the in-laws, houses with picket fences, children, and grandchildren. The only thing that mattered to me then — the only thing that matters to me still — is that Jimmy Dean was my kind of guy.

★ ★ ★

Teen Idol

I USED TO BE TEDDIE-BOY, YOU KNOW, the lovable but mischievous teenage son on *Four and the Folks*. The cute one with the big eyes, with the depth. Billy and Bobby didn't have any depth, and let's face it, Mandy-Sue was a dog.

I was Teddie-Boy. Come on, don't tell me you don't know Teddie-Boy. I also had a singing career, *two number one* songs, darling. And two number three songs, too, for the record. I didn't have a great voice or anything, I'm not bragging here, I wasn't any Elvis. But I had . . . what's the word . . . a *charismatic* voice. Anyway, you'll know the songs — "Teen Idol's Love" and "Merry-Go-Round Mary (She Broke My Heart)." Come on! Those were the two number ones, not the number threes!

No? Really? You're kidding me, putting me on, pulling

my leg, right? You don't recognize either of them? And you don't remember the show either? It ran for *five* years. I'm not bragging here, but five years ain't peanuts. They're constantly talking syndication deals, and one of these days, you'll see, it'll happen.

No, no, I'm not being hostile to you, I most certainly am not, excuse me if something about my manner gives you that impression. Of course you don't remember the show or the songs. Why *should* you? You're absolutely right, there's no reason, since it's obvious, just as you point out, that you really are *very* young, far too young to remember.

Yes, yes, it's my fault. All my fault. I didn't realize how young you were. No, don't take offense. I'm not saying you don't *look* young. In fact, you look *very, very* young, like a high school cheerleader, I swear you do. A little bit like Mandy-Sue was supposed to look on *Four and the Folks,* if she hadn't looked like a dog instead.

No, come on, *you're* no dog, that's not what I'm saying. You're terrific looking, and *very, very* young. Not a line on your face. Not a wrinkle on your neck. You're so blond, your skin looks so soft, your breasts — shown off to great advantage, I must say, in that black little number you've got on tonight — look so high, so firm. And, real, too, am I right? I thought so. Anyway, that's why I started talking to you here at the bar in the first place. Your youth. Your blond hair. Your breasts.

No, sorry, darling, I'm not being obnoxious, well, maybe I am, but I don't mean to be. What I mean is that it's hard for me, sometimes, to remember that not everyone knows Teddie-Boy, that's all. It's hard for me to remember that I'm not as young as I was. It's *my* problem, not yours. Definitely my problem.

Here, let me order you another — what is it you're

drinking? Right, another *Virgin* Sea Breeze for this *very, very* young, very blond lady by my side, with the high and firm and real breasts. . . . Sorry again, no more comments about your breasts, I promise, on Teddie-Boy's honor.

And, hey, if that's the way you like it, a Virgin Sea Breeze, no liquor, okay, it's not for me to say. You say virgin, virgin's just fine with me. Me, however, no virgin here — I'll have another double Scotch. Straight up.

Speaking of virginity, let me tell you, I lost mine at twelve years old, with the so-called talent scout who discovered me, a third cousin of my mother. She saw me singing at my school assembly. Two weeks later, she popped my cherry. No, I'm not bragging. It wasn't any great shakes. It was much better with Tessa Von Turndaale, who played Mom on *Four and the Folks,* and who helped me land the role of Teddie-Boy in the first place. There also were some steamy nights with Dahlia Smith, the bisexual dominatrix who played the role of Nancy, the sweet baby-sitter who lived next door, and okay, even once, at a drunken party, I confess, with Mandy-Sue, the dog, but never, never with Kirkie Small, who played Billy, like some of the rumors had it. On the show, though, I had to act like I didn't even know how babies were made, like a kiss on the lips was enough to turn Teddie-Boy's world upside down — bullshit in spades, if you get my drift. But I could really act, and believe me, kids everywhere were convinced that Teddie-Boy's li'l old pecker was pure as the virgin snow.

So, anyway, like I said — cheers and down the hatch — I was Teddie-Boy. A major heartthrob. Big league. On the cover of every teen mag. Fans mobbed me wherever I went. I bet your mother remembers me. Go on, ask her. I'll give you a quarter to call her. Go ahead. Call her right now. Okay, okay, I'm not trying to force you. Forget it. But sometime, just ask her, you'll see. Say, "Hey, Mom, didn't you want to screw old Teddie-Boy back when you were growing up?"

No, no, I swear, I am *not* being hostile. I *love* your mother. In fact, I love your whole family — a lot more than I loved my TV family on *Four and the Folks,* or my own mother and father, who both drank themselves to death by the time I was twenty.

Anyway, the main thing is that one day, just like that, we were canceled. Still, I wasn't worried. Why should I have been? I felt on top of the world. Because you see, darling, here's what I believed, eighteen-year-old sucker that I was: I believed that I wasn't just Teddie-Boy. I believed that it was *me* the fans loved. I believed that my fans were loyal. After all, I was the one on the show who had the singing career. I'd already proved myself out in the world, right? Billy and Bobby didn't have hit songs, or Mandy-Sue the dog, or Dahlia Smith, who, by the way, is now one of the highest-paid dominatrixes in L.A.

But I was wrong. Agents wouldn't return my calls. Producers wouldn't let me read for parts. Record companies turned deaf ears. I was "overidentified" with Teddie-Boy, they said. But I didn't even know what the word meant. "Overidentified?" I asked, dumb eighteen-year-old hotshot kid that I was. "What's that?" "It means," my agent explained to me, "you don't exist. Only Teddie-Boy exists. And Teddie-Boy, rest his soul, is dead." "Kaput," my mother's third cousin, the talent scout, told me. "Has-been."

So who could blame me? You won't, darling, I know that. I fell apart. I drank. I took drugs. I was eighteen, maybe a year or two younger than you are right now, and already *kaput,* already a *has-been,* already *overidentified.*

No, no, I'm not trying to get you to tell me your age. As far as I'm concerned, you're sweet sixteen, a cheerleader with high and firm and real breasts forever, so don't worry. That's not my point. My point is that I was already used to having lots and lots of money, fast cars, fast women. So I began to hang out with a bunch of other ex–teen idols, other *over-identified* has-beens, like Louie from *Prairie Family* and Mitch from *Rockin' Junior High*. We were angry, hurt, confused. We had no skills, no high school diplomas. All we knew was showbiz. So we robbed, cheated, scammed, and even scored tricks now and then. We were furious. But guilt? No, no guilt at all. After all, we were just doing to others what had been done to us first. *We'd* been robbed—of our whole lives. Other people had identities. We had none. When Teddie-Boy was canceled, so was I.

Then we were contacted by some old farts, these guys in their forties and fifties, and believe me, darling, forty seemed like an old fart to me then—all former teen idols. They contacted us when we made the papers, that time we were caught robbing the gas station. "We can help you," they said to me and Louie and Mitch. They called themselves "Teen Idols Aging Together," and their motto was "Overidentified But Not Over!" They arranged for us to meet them in a dark church basement. They were all wearing gold chains and polyester shirts. They told us they were now "self-actualized" and "thriving," with "real careers," like selling real estate and used cars. But back when their shows were first canceled, they said, they too had robbed, cheated, scammed, and scored. But they had good lives now, they swore, between their real careers, their AA meetings, and the bleached-blond wives they'd all met at AA. They invited us to visit them at home. Their houses were filled with all their old stuff. Gold records. Photos of them shaking hands with Elvis. Cute little gifts sent by their long-extinct fan clubs. "Hey," I said, "if you guys don't care about being teen idols any more, why all this stuff?" "It's not that we miss those days, son," they said. "We just *acknowledge* them, that's all." They were one group of lying, pathetic old farts, let me tell you, darling. "Better to forget those days as Teddie-Boy," they advised me. "Better for you to move on. Get some skills. Take a course in real estate, or bookkeeping. Join us. You're one of us. Nobody will ever understand you the way we understand you. We were Pookster Jr. on *Pookster Rogers & Son,* and Little Ed on *Air Force Family,* and Chambers Carter Randall III, the rich-but-lovable kid on *Townies,*" they said, as though that would cement the bonds between us forever.

But I fled from them and their gold chains and their real estate courses. They may have convinced Louie and Mitch, but not me! I wasn't one of them. I was the greatest teen idol of them all! I wasn't just Pookster Jr. or Little Ed, and I sure wasn't Chambers Carter Randall III! I was Teddie-Boy on *Four and the Folks.* I had two number one songs, and two number three songs. I'm as good as ever. I'll make my come-back yet. You'll see.

What is it, darling? You're laughing at me? Crying for me? Well, no matter, there's no need for either. Come on, let's have another double Scotch, and another Virgin Sea Breeze. Cheers and down the hatch. Here's to Teddie-Boy. Here's to me. We live.

★ ★ ★

The Princess of Lake Forest

T HE YEAR THAT *The Princess Kitty Kat Show* debuted on TV, I was ten, and my sister Beth was twelve. Beth, who was wild-tempered, hated *The Princess Kitty Kat Show.* "Constance," she would say angrily to me, "you're so naive, liking a show about dumb animals. No dumb animal could ever be a princess!" In spite of Beth, the Saturday afternoon cartoon about the adventures of Princess Kitty Kat of the Kingdom of Felineia quickly became my favorite TV show.

Or perhaps, I realize now, almost two decades later, it was *because* of Beth's hatred for the teenaged Princess Kitty Kat that I adored her so much.

Princess Kitty Kat was a curly-haired, green-eyed Siamese who walked upright and wore a glittering crown and floor-length gowns and capes. Princess Kitty Kat was dating a commoner cat, a rugged, handsome tom named Whiskers. The king and queen of Felineia, Princess Kitty Kat's parents, were always concocting schemes to try to break them up. To add to the delicious complications, Pussette, the raven-haired, evil witch cat, hated Princess Kitty Kat and wanted to steal Whiskers away from her.

I was pretty sure that the real reason Beth hated Princess Kitty Kat was because Beth thought of herself as a fairy-tale princess, and she didn't want any competition, not even from a cartoon. I was no competition for Beth. I had dark and unruly hair, an olive complexion, and sharp, exaggerated features. Still, Beth would frequently slap me, punch me, and pull my hair, usually for no reason that I could understand. My mother admitted that Beth had "violent spells." "But," she added, sipping her ever-present vodka martini, "how can anyone stay mad at such a pretty little princess?" Beth looked very much the way my mother had looked as a little girl in the photographs my mother kept out on her bureau, with the same silky blond hair, long-lashed, aqua-colored eyes, and peaches-and-cream complexion, which, depending on the light, was sometimes more peaches, and sometimes more cream.

In addition to *The Princess Kitty Kat Show*, Beth also hated my best friend, Angela. In Angela's case, I figured it was because Angela's father, a Chicago real-estate entrepreneur, had made millions, and so Angela lived in an even wealthier part of Lake Forest than we did: The houses were bigger, the gardens more lush, and the mothers sometimes drove their Rolls Royces into town just to go to the beauty parlor.

Despite her family's money, Angela, like me, was no competition for Beth. Her hair was a mousy color, her small brown eyes were too close together, and her pale lips too thin. I loved Angela in spite of Beth, or — as with Princess Kitty Kat — perhaps because of her.

"Constance, do you think that you could ever fall in love with a poor man?" Angela asked me one Saturday afternoon, after we'd just watched an episode of *The Princess Kitty Kat Show* together.

I was sitting on Angela's mother's spotless white sofa, and I gingerly crossed my legs before answering. "Sure, I could love a poor man."

"How can you be so sure?" Angela pursued. She was standing barefoot in front of the TV, on the spotless white rug that matched the sofa. She turned off the TV and stared intently at me.

I stared back at her, surprised. "Well, because I believe that everyone is equal, rich or poor. Don't you?"

"I guess so." Angela looked down at the white rug. "But it doesn't really matter what I believe, because my mother would never, never let me be with a poor man! Never."

Before I could try to convince Angela that she, like Princess Kitty Kat, was entitled to her own beliefs, the maid came in to clean, and Angela and I were sent upstairs to Angela's room, where we sat and played Steal the Old Man's Bundle, our favorite card game, until it was time for Angela's dance lesson.

Because of my love for *The Princess Kitty Kat Show*, I began craving a cat of my very own. I knew, though, that it would be difficult to convince my mother to let me have a cat. For one thing, she didn't especially like animals. And for another, it wasn't easy getting through to her at all: She'd been a heavy drinker ever since my father, at that time a corporate lawyer in Chicago, had — in incredibly rapid fashion — left her for another woman, moved to Florida, become a self-professed "swinger," and died of pancreatic cancer, all before I'd even entered kindergarten. I didn't know all the details then. I knew only that my father had left us, and that he had died soon after. And that my mother drank.

Still, I was determined to have a cat. "Mother, I want a cat more than anything in the whole world," I kept telling her. I was careful to say this only when Beth wasn't around. I didn't want her putting her two cents in. I wanted something that would be mine alone, that Beth wouldn't be able to touch.

At first my mother refused even to consider the possibility. "Constance," she would say, "it's enough trouble having two girls in the house. I don't need animals, too." Sometimes she seemed so high, she spoke as though she weren't even sure what she was saying, as though her words were abstract objects with no meaning. Other times, she seemed melancholy, as though she were thinking that if only things had turned out differently, she would have loved to have been the sort of mother who welcomed the company of children and pets, rather than finding them burdensome.

But one Saturday afternoon, with no warning and no explanation, my mother returned from doing errands in town, holding a tiny black kitten in her arms. "Promise me you'll clean out her box every single day," she said.

"I promise! I promise!" I could barely believe my good fortune. Eagerly, I held out my arms to take the kitten from her.

"I mean it," she went on, not relinquishing the kitten, who'd begun meowing loudly. "I almost lost my life on account of this cat."

I continued to wait for her to let me hold the kitten. Finally, she placed the kitten in my outstretched arms.

I held the fragile kitten gently, lifting her close to my face. Deliriously, I inhaled her exotic animal smell.

Pouring herself a drink from the well-stocked bar, my

mother proceeded to tell me in great detail about how, because she'd been so distracted by the kitten's incessant meowing, she'd been in a car accident on the way home from the pet shop, but, luckily, nobody had been injured and the car wasn't damaged.

"Mother," I said, waiting patiently until she had finished, "giving me this kitten is a good and kind thing! I'll love you forever for this!"

She looked fuzzily at me over the rim of her highball glass. "You're an interesting one," she said, smiling slightly. From her, that was a great compliment, since she couldn't say that I looked like a princess.

I kissed the furry little kitten. "I'm going to name her Princess Kitty Kat!"

"Princess Kitty Kat?" my mother asked. "What kind of a name is that?"

"Oh, Mother, you know, it's the cartoon cat." I was excited, because *The Princess Kitty Kat Show* was scheduled to be on soon, and that seemed a marvelous coincidence, an auspicious omen for my life to come with the black kitten.

I fed the kitten some milk, played with her, and began teaching her to respond to her name. When the show came on, I held her in front of the TV set. When the cartoon Princess Kitty Kat danced a regal-looking dance, with court-seys and mincing little steps, I had my own Princess Kitty Kat do a version of the dance, too. When the show's theme song played—"Princess Kitty Kat's a fancy cat!/A royal cat!/A cat who sings and dances like *THAT!*"—I sang along, softly.

My mother, drink in hand, looked in on us. "Here, kitty, kitty," she called. But Princess Kitty Kat didn't look over at her. She sat in my lap, purring, looking up only at me.

When the show was finished, I telephoned Angela and invited her to come over to meet Princess Kitty Kat.

Angela biked right over. "She's nice," she said, petting her head.

"Oh, Angela," I cried, with uncharacteristic passion, "she's not just *nice!* She's beautiful, wonderful, the best cat in the whole world!"

Beth didn't come home until after dinner. She'd been at a classmate's all-day birthday party. "There was a really awful band," she announced to nobody in particular as she walked into the house, "and a rotten-tasting cake!"

I was sitting on the sofa. Princess Kitty Kat sat calmly on my lap, licking her tiny black paws.

"What's that?" Beth yelled, coming into the living room in her pink, ruffled party dress, her silky blond hair held neatly in place by velvet ribbons.

"My cat," I said, nervously but defiantly. "Her name is Princess Kitty Kat."

Beth squinted her aqua-colored eyes at Princess Kitty Kat. Then she ran into the garden. "Take her back," she shouted at my mother, who was sitting in the fading light, playing bridge and sharing a pitcher of vodka martinis with a few of her girlfriends. I followed closely behind, my heart racing, clinging tightly to Princess Kitty Kat.

My mother appeared embarrassed in front of her friends by Beth's willfulness. "Beth," she said, "go to your room!" My mother rarely stood up to Beth, and I was certain that if she had anticipated Beth's reaction, she never would have gotten me the cat.

I remained in the garden, too terrified to move, clutching a squirming Princess Kitty Kat in my arms, as Beth stalked off to her room in a rage, and my mother tried to smooth things over with her friends by freshening everyone's drink.

One Sunday afternoon, after I'd had Princess Kitty Kat for about three months, Angela and I were in my bedroom, playing Steal the Old Man's Bundle and laughing happily whenever Princess Kitty Kat pounced on the deck and tried to join the game. About two o'clock, after we'd been playing for a couple of hours, we grew hungry, and I offered to make us ice-cream sundaes.

I went into the kitchen, and I felt very grown up as I neatly put out the necessary items on the counter: bowls, spoons, container of vanilla ice cream, ice-cream scoop, chocolate syrup, chocolate sprinkles, whipped cream, and walnuts. Softly humming the theme song from *The Princess Kitty Kat Show,* I began spooning the ice cream into the bowls.

I was nearly at the final stage of pouring on the chocolate syrup when Beth came through the swinging doors. She was wearing pale pink shorts, a white cotton blouse with a Peter Pan collar, and thin, ladylike sandals on her feet. Dramatically, flinging her arms around like a stage actress, she said, "Constance, I advise you to put aside your childish little sundaes, and to come down to the basement with me, where your friend Angela awaits you!"

I licked some chocolate syrup off my fingers. "Angela's not in the basement," I said with exaggerated calm. "Angela's in my room."

"Come down to the basement," Beth repeated, tossing back her blond hair, "if you know what's good for you!"

Bewildered, I wiped my hands on my blue jeans and followed Beth downstairs, wishing my mother hadn't gone out to plant flowers with her garden club.

Angela was seated on top of the rusty toolbox my father had left behind, and which, along with his tools, my mother had never bothered to get rid of. There were ropes tied tightly across Angela's wrists and ankles. One of my mother's perfumed, lavender silk handkerchiefs served as a gag over her mouth. I stared disbelievingly at Angela, whose close-set, brown eyes were wide with terror. I couldn't even begin to imagine what horrible lies Beth must have told in order to get Angela down to the basement and into such a position.

Beth picked up a screwdriver and held it to Angela's throat. "Put the cat out on the street," she ordered me, "or your friend here dies." She smiled.

I felt sick. I continued to stare at Angela, who was wearing a yellow playsuit with bows at the waist. She'd begun whimpering.

Turning my back on them both, I began running up the basement stairs. All I wanted was to get away, fast. My heart was racing, and I was having trouble breathing.

Beth stood at the bottom of the stairs. "I'll kill her!" she called up to me. "I really will!"

I turned around at the top of the stairs. "You'll get caught," I said. My voice trembled, and I gasped for air. I was mortified by my own cowardice. The last thing I should have been doing was running away. I should have been fighting Beth on Angela's behalf. But I couldn't. I was just too frightened.

"Fat chance!" Beth shouted back. "My plan is foolproof! And the best part is that I'm going to say that *you* did it." She began to laugh. "I'll blame *you,* Constance. You'll hang! And I'll stand there laughing, watching you swinging in the breeze."

Angela's whimpers grew louder. Still gasping for air, I ran upstairs to my bedroom. Princess Kitty Kat was fast asleep on my windowsill, basking in the bright mid-afternoon sunlight. I lay on my bed, watching her. The sunlight began to make me feel sleepy, as well, and I longed to be able to give in, to fall asleep and block out the image of what was taking place down below in the basement.

Beth opened my door, startling me out of my half-sleep. My mother didn't allow us to have locks on our doors. "You've got one more hour to put that thing out on the street," Beth pointed at Princess Kitty Kat, still blissfully asleep on the windowsill, "or Angela dies!" She slammed the door. Lying there in the sunlight, on the verge of sleep, I felt even more ashamed of my fear and weakness.

Princess Kitty Kat awoke. She trotted over to me on the bed, nuzzling against me, offering me her belly to stroke. "I love you, I love you," I repeated over and over to her, marveling at her shiny black fur and her soft body, wondering at the same time what terrible and cruel things Beth was saying to Angela down in the basement, wondering why this was happening at all, why Beth would even want to do such a thing. I understood that Angela and Princess Kitty Kat were both just pawns, and that it was really me that Beth was after, me she really wanted to hurt. But what I couldn't understand was why Beth hated me so much.

I envisioned Beth slitting Angela's throat with my father's rusty screwdriver and chopping her body into tiny pieces with his old electric saw. "I love you," I said even more passionately to Princess Kitty Kat, desperately wishing that she could help me. Beth opened my door a second time, chortling, "Your time is running out!" She ran off again.

I stared at the clock on my bureau. Princess Kitty Kat, curled up against me, was looking directly into my eyes, which made me feel even more confused and helpless. Perhaps all sisters did such nasty things to each other, I thought, and I was just a silly little baby, making a big deal over nothing.

I closed my eyes to avoid Princess Kitty Kat's unblinking, trusting gaze. No, I didn't believe that Beth was merely a nasty girl. Beth's actions were monstrous. I had to face the truth about my sister, or at least, the truth about this monstrous being who called herself my sister. Beth was truly wicked. Beth was just like Pussette, the cartoon witch cat who committed evil deeds every Saturday afternoon in the Kingdom of Felineia just for the sheer thrill of doing evil. Although the knowledge of who — or *what* — Beth really was, chilled and horrified me, it also gave me newfound strength and courage, because I knew at last the truth of what I was dealing with.

I planted a sorrowful kiss on Princess Kitty Kat's head, and I forced myself to walk back down the creaky stairs to the basement. Beth and Angela both watched me as I descended the stairs. "Let her go," I said, standing in front of Angela, whose eyes were bloodshot from crying. The handkerchief over her mouth was soaked. "Let her go, Beth! I'll tell Mother to find another home for Princess Kitty Kat."

"No," Beth said, shaking her head so that her blond hair bounced, "that's not good enough, Constance. The cat goes out on the street. Now!"

"I hate you, Beth," I said. "I know your secret. I know that you're evil, through and through. And I will never, never forgive you for what you have done today." I spoke calmly. I had had enough. I was prepared to fight Beth if I had to. My hands were shaking as I began untying the ropes. Beth stood still, watching me.

When Angela was free, I lowered my eyes in shame, assuming that she also now hated me because I hadn't rescued her earlier, because I had vacillated and shown such weakness. I wouldn't have blamed her. "I'm sorry, Angel," I said. It was a nickname I'd heard her mother use, but which I'd never used before. To my surprise, though, she thanked me through her tears. She even squeezed my hand, before running up the basement stairs and out of the house, never looking back. I remember noticing that the seat of her yellow playsuit was wet, and I didn't blame her for that, either.

Slowly, I walked up the basement stairs, wondering whether Beth was going to attack me from behind, but she didn't. Still shaking, I went into the kitchen and threw out the melted ice-cream sundaes. I rinsed the bowls and placed them in the dishwasher. When the kitchen was neat enough not to anger my mother, I went back to my bedroom, put away the deck of playing cards, and lay down next to Princess Kitty Kat, who was fast asleep again. I felt spent and defeated. I expected Beth to barge in, but she never did.

At dinner that evening, I spoke as calmly as I could. "Mother," I said, "I don't want the cat any longer." I knew that I had no choice but to get Princess Kitty Kat out of the house, before Beth tried to harm her directly.

"May I ask why?" My mother was sober for a change, and clearly exasperated with me.

"Cats are too much work," I lied.

My mother didn't say anything. Beth stared smugly at me.

"I really don't like cats," I lied again.

"Well, Constance, don't ever ask me again for a pet of any kind, do you hear me?" my mother said, her voice rising, her cheeks growing red. "Not a dog or a bird or even a fish or a hamster. Do you hear?"

I avoided Beth's smug stare. I nodded. "Please, just be sure to find Princess Kitty Kat a good home." I hoped my voice wouldn't break. "Please!"

Within a couple of days, my mother, who was on a short-lived sobriety kick, announced that she had, indeed, found a new — "and better," as she put it — home for Princess Kitty Kat. The fourteen-year-old son of one of her bridge partners had been wanting a black cat for a while.

I was horrified, but I held back my tears. I'd heard unsettling rumors about this boy, that there was something not quite right about him, that the girls his age all kept their distance from him. I watched helplessly from my window as my mother drove off to Lake Bluff to bring Princess Kitty Kat to her new home. "What can I do to help Princess Kitty Kat?" I said aloud. I felt small and powerless.

Beth, who was in her bedroom next door, began singing the theme song from *The Princess Kitty Kat Show* at the top of her lungs. I clenched my fists in rage. I wanted to go next door and rip her tongue from her throat, but I knew that if I did, I would be no better than she was, that I would be committing evil, myself.

I had to accept the fact that there was nothing I could do to bring Princess Kitty Kat back to me, but perhaps there *was* something I could do, after all, to combat Beth's evil. As soon as I was old enough, I would move someplace far, far away from Lake Forest, far away from the evil Beth and my alcoholic mother, and even, sadly, far away from timid Angela. And there, in that other place—a place that was nothing like Lake Forest—I would dedicate myself, for the rest of my life, to helping the poor, the lonely, the sick, and the needy. For every evil deed that Beth performed, I would perform a good one. And I would never, never return to Lake Forest. I unclenched my fists, turned away from the window, and climbed into bed, where, smiling, I put a pillow over my head to block out the sound of Beth's singing.

★ ★ ★

And now, here in Berkeley — a place that is nothing like Lake Forest — where I've lived alone for almost two decades, I lie awake in my narrow bed in the middle of the night, unable to sleep. My three cats are nuzzling me, competing for my attention. One is a flirty calico, one a white, blue-eyed deaf cat, and one a scrappy grey tom. I rescued them all from the streets. I stroke them carefully, one by one, making sure to give them equal attention, although I feel utterly exhausted from a long day at the clinic where I counsel teenage girls, girls like Laticia who slit her wrists and almost died on the day she first learned she was pregnant.

I listen to the drug dealers down below on Telegraph Avenue, fighting and cursing among themselves, and I stare up at the yellowing ceiling over my bed. Still stroking the cats, I find myself thinking of Beth, to whom I speak briefly on the phone each Christmas, but at no other time. I picture her with the handsome, wealthy man she married shortly after they both graduated from Lake Forest College. I imagine the two of them, and their two teenaged sons, sitting down together in their elegant dining room in their huge Victorian house, only blocks away from the house in which we grew up, the house in which my mother died five years ago in her sleep, leaving most of her money to Beth.

I picture Beth and her family sitting down to a hearty meal prepared by their cook: a crisp, fresh salad; a thick, oozing steak smothered in brown gravy; and hot, buttered bread. I grow more and more awake, and more and more enraged, and the picture grows more and more specific: Beth's husband and sons watching her with adoration as she sips expensive red wine from a shimmering, crystal goblet, as she regales them with charming anecdotes about her afternoon shopping in town.

What enrages me most is that Beth, the bad sister, is rich and happy. She's well loved by her family, and by the many women friends with whom she gardens and shops. One of her best friends is Angela, also married, also still in Lake Forest.

And yet Constance, the good sister, lives all alone, too frightened — too "damaged," they call it in her social work textbooks — to grow close to anyone.

I rise from the bed, throw a robe over my shoulders, and walk to the window. I look out into the night, through the slats of the heavy window gates that I use for protection from robbers and rapists. My cats follow me, curling themselves around my bare ankles. None of this is my fault, I assure myself. Beth and I were just two unhappy little girls, coping in the only ways we could: Beth, by doing mischief; me, by striving to be perfect. If our father hadn't left us, if my mother had joined AA, well then, Beth and I would have been much happier little girls. Really, it's very clear-cut. I've turned out just fine. What more can I expect? Life can't be a fairy tale, no matter how much an unhappy little girl may wish it to be.

I turn away from the window and return to bed. All three cats follow me. I lie rigidly, shutting my eyes tight. But I'm too enraged to fall asleep, because deep inside I'm *still* that unhappy little girl who believed in *Cinderella, Snow White,* and *Sleeping Beauty,* who believed that the sweet and good Princess Kitty Kat of Felineia would defeat the bitchy and evil Pussette, and that good little girls everywhere lived happily ever after.

Finally, lying there sleepless, I understand what it is that keeps me awake. It's that, deep down, what I really believe is this: The fault lies inside of me. It *must*. It must be that Constance, the good sister, will never, never be good enough, no matter where she may live, no matter what she may do, no matter how hard she may try.

Then I sit up in bed. I turn on the light. The cats stare at me, their eyes aglow and curious. "*No,*" I say aloud, "I *am* good. I am kind. I have been constant." I am, after all, the princess who grew up in the Land of Lake Forest. And even though I am not recognized in my own land, my reward will be in the deeds that I do.

★ ★ ★

The Ping-Pong Vampire

U NLESS YOU TRAVEL IN CERTAIN circles, I'm sure you've never heard of me. But not too long ago, I did have a pretty big reputation in my field. In those days, I wrote treatises on sports and games. My best-known book was *The Semiotics of Softball*. Whenever I was asked why, as a female, I'd been drawn to the world of sports, I answered that there was a hidden language in sports just ripe for decoding. I compared myself to an Egyptologist, obsessively deciphering ancient drawings. I spoke of a love of language, of a burning desire to unearth the hidden meanings of symbols, the buried subtexts of texts.

But that was all a big fat lie. The truth, which I never told anyone, was that I had a thing about jocks. I just loved their sweaty, mesomorphic, hunky bodies—their tight butts, thick necks, and muscular thighs. This is one of the dreams I used to have back then: I'm standing in the middle of the male locker room after a game. The smell of victory is in the air. The guys are all naked, swinging their towels around, smacking each other jubilantly on their buns. I'm wearing only a black, lacy garter belt, black stockings, and black high heels. I'm delirious from the odor of soiled jockstraps, wet towels, and sweaty flesh. Then, jock after jock flings me down on the locker room bench and makes love to me. They all follow exactly the same athletic rhythm, as though there's been a huddle beforehand. They're gentle, they're rough, and then they're gentle again. And, together, we score a mutual touchdown.

Believe me, I knew that these dreams really were all about my submitting to a bunch of insensitive brutes. But I felt entitled to whatever fantasy life I wanted. Since sexual fantasies, like myths and fairy tales, were a part of the collective unconscious, why should I be held singularly accountable for dreams shared by so many women?

In real life, though, I had nothing in common with the jocks. In high school, I once overheard Davey Smith, the captain of the football team, say to Petey Grofer, the quarterback, "Rowena Ardsley? She's got no tits, no legs. She's a walking encyclopedia, that one." Petey Grofer laughed, and the nickname took. I became known as the Walking Encyclopedia, a nickname I rather liked. Mostly, I stayed home alone, worrying about what I would do for a living when I got out of school, how I would reconcile my braininess with my fantasies of jocks.

★ ★ ★

In college, though, things fell into place: I began writing term papers in which I deconstructed the games that the jocks played. My professors were impressed, not having any idea that for me, writing those papers was like writing erotic prose, that it was a sensual experience. At night, before I fell asleep, I read my own papers aloud to myself, and then I dreamed my locker room dreams all night long.

I wasn't unattractive. I had nice features, and thick red hair that I kept pinned up in a bun. I wore classic, tortoiseshell eyeglasses. I had a quiet beauty, like the prim, bespectacled nurse in that old movie, *The Interns*. The one who, during the hospital's Christmas party, removes her eyeglasses, lets down her hair, and reveals herself as a wild sexpot. Really, though, I didn't have any desire to do the same. Except in my dreams, of course, which I took no responsibility for.

After graduate school, I became a college teacher. A few years later, I was awarded tenure. Then, out of the blue, I was invited to take a year off from teaching to become a member of the Sports, Games, and Toys Institute, a brand-new think tank located somewhere in the mountains of North Carolina. The institute was a purely commercial venture. A group of scientists, scholars, doctors, artists, and journalists would all live together for a year in a large house. A staff would serve us our meals and clean our rooms. We would be paid a large stipend. All we were being asked to do was to invent as many new games, toys, and sports-related items as we could, all of which were intended to become huge moneymakers for Game-i-Con, the conglomerate that was sponsoring the institute. Game-i-Con was desperate to compete with the Japanese, who, rumor had it, were about to enter the sports, games, and toys industry with the same fervor with which they'd previously entered the electronics industry.

I hesitated to accept the offer. I was used to my quiet life: teaching, writing books, dreaming about jocks. I didn't even attend sports events in person. I watched them on TV instead, because I was too afraid of losing my self-control. I certainly didn't have the slightest desire to go off and live with a bunch of strangers. But my department chairman loved the idea. He thought it would be prestigious, and he pressured me to accept. So, reluctantly, I packed my bags, and I flew down south. I fell asleep on the plane, and the entire way there I dreamed of garter belts and jockstraps.

★ ★ ★

To my surprise, though, I settled in quickly to life at the institute. There were fifteen of us altogether: eight men and seven women, all unmarried and childless, each of us a specialist, each obsessed with our own particular specialty. I hadn't been the only one in that group who'd been known as the Walking Encylopedia back in high school.

Days at the institute were easy and routine. We spent the mornings brainstorming around the long marble table in the conference room on the main floor. Then, after lunch, we'd break up into committees. I was on the language committee. Our goal was to come up with new, catchy names for old games, in order to convince people that the old games were brand-new.

After dinner, we'd break up into various groups and entertain ourselves for the rest of the evening. I joined the Ping-Pong group. We would head downstairs to the musty basement where there was a wobbly Ping-Pong table. None of us knew how to slam the ball, or even how to put spin on it, and so we'd play a few noncompetitive, unathletic games.

Finally, after Ping-Pong, I'd climb up those steep stairs to my bedroom. I'd change into my flimsy white nightgown, and I'd lie in bed and read aloud excerpts from my own books, until, in a kind of erotic reverie, I'd fall asleep, and I'd dream my dreams of submission and domination in the locker room.

★ ★ ★

After about three months of this routine, Game-i-Con's CEO—who dropped by periodically for progress reports—announced that a new member was coming to the institute. None of us were thrilled by his news. We were a pretty stodgy bunch, not the sort who welcomed change.

The new member's name, we were told by the CEO, was Byron Ravage. He was a Ping-Pong champion. He was also a poet, and he had written a book called *The Ping-Pong Poems.* "Byron Ravage is a true Renaissance man," the CEO said, passing around a glossy head shot of a brooding man with shiny black hair to his shoulders. He wore mirrored, aviator sunglasses with metal frames. His lips were thin, angry lines. He looked skinny and tense, wired to explode.

I took an instant dislike to the face in that photo. He didn't look like the rest of us. He looked too cool, or too hip, or whatever. His Ping-Pong poems were probably sloppy little verses, not at all rigorous. This was not the face of a man who could compose a sonnet or a sestina. I wasn't impressed.

Lucas Smith, who was known for his invention of a Frankenstein doll that made terrifying gutteral sounds, also seemed to take an instant dislike to Byron Ravage's photo. Lucas, who was religious, began fingering the cross around his neck, and muttering something that sounded like, "And so, the beast returns," but I couldn't be sure.

All I knew for sure was that I wasn't looking forward to Byron Ravage's arrival. I hoped that he wasn't going to volunteer to be on the Language Committee. I also hoped that he wouldn't join our tepid little Ping-Pong group. Maybe, instead, he would join the group that watched the evening news on TV. Or the group — which included Lucas Smith —that watched films every night on the VCR. Or the group that drank themselves into a stupor, night after night, in front of the fireplace in the living room. Or, perhaps, best of all, he'd keep to himself.

★ ★ ★

Just as I feared, after Byron Ravage's arrival, the atmosphere changed. First of all, his physical presence was unnerving: he always wore those off-putting sunglasses, and he always dressed in black. What had been such a pleasant atmosphere became an unpleasant, sexually charged one. Helenska, for example, a fortyish blonde who was an illustrator of sports figures, began dressing in low-cut sequined gowns. Quite frankly, I'd never thought that Helenska was really brainy enough for the institute, and now I was certain of it. And Gertrude, a retired German scientist, began telling bawdy jokes in a loud voice at mealtimes.

Helenska and Gertrude, and all of the other women, as well, wanted to go to bed with Byron Ravage. Their lust for him embarrassed me. I never fantasized about him. He was no jock. Ping-Pong was just too namby-pamby a game for my taste. A little green table, a little white ball, a little low net. Why, anyone could play Ping-Pong! Even *I* could get the ball over the net now and then. I didn't believe that Byron Ravage would have had the strength to throw me down on a locker room bench if he *wanted* to.

The men at the institute, unlike the women, all seemed to hate him. On sight and instinctively. As though he were some sort of threat to them. Lucas Smith, for instance, always gnashed his teeth, muttered under his breath, and fingered his cross whenever Byron walked by.

I assured myself, though, that neither the women's lust, nor the men's hatred, had anything to do with me. I didn't like the man, sure, but what was the big deal? I would just keep on thinking up new names for old games. I hadn't had much success, though. All I'd come up with were pockethole ball for nok hockey, and netracket for tennis.

One night before dinner, a couple of weeks after he'd arrived, Byron Ravage announced that he would give a poetry reading that evening. I'd pretty much avoided him up until that point. I never sat at his table at mealtimes. And, luckily, he hadn't joined the language committee. In fact, he'd told everyone he wanted to wait a bit before he decided upon a committee. Which, I think, relieved all the men, and disappointed all the other women. Also, he'd proved to be a loner, which meant that I could stick to my nightly routine of a few tepid games of Ping-Pong. I really didn't want to break up my routine to attend his little performance. But finally I decided it would be too rude not to.

After dinner, Byron, wearing his mirrored sunglasses, a pair of tight black jeans, and a black sweater, pulled up a chair for himself in front of the fire. The men gathered in a group, pulling their chairs close together, way in the back, as far from Byron as possible. They gnashed their teeth, muttered, and frowned a lot. Lucas Smith chomped ferociously on a cigar, although I'd never seen him smoke before.

All of the women, except for me, gathered together in a cluster on the rug. They sat as close as possible to Byron, without actually climbing into his lap. They preened, sighed, rolled their eyes, licked their lips, and smiled seductively at him. Helenska wore her lowest-cut gown yet, a pink, frothy, floor-length affair. Gertrude had put a blue rinse in her hair, and was wearing pearls around her neck.

I sat in the middle, between the two groups, on the rug, resting my head on my knees. I felt apart and separate from both groups, almost as though, at that moment, I was neither male nor female. Nor human at all. As though I belonged to some whole other species. And, just when I had that thought, I looked up and saw Byron Ravage staring right at me, with such an intense look that I had the strange sensation that he was reading my mind. And that he approved of what he read.

"I'm not going to read from *The Ping-Pong Poems.*" Byron spoke in a smooth, velvety voice, turning his attention away from me. He skillfully managed to make eye contact with each and every one of us while he spoke, working the room like an old Las Vegas pro. "Since I think you all need a break from sports metaphors," he grinned, "I'm going to read a poem of mine that has no need for metaphors at all." He began to recite an old-fashioned ballad about a woman with blue eyes, dark hair, and bright red lips, and how this woman meets a mysterious stranger who dresses all in black and who has glimmering white teeth, which he eventually sinks into the skin of her long neck, and how both of them are then transformed into eternal, vampire lovers. There was one catchy stanza that he kept reciting throughout: "Vampire / Do It / Bite Me / Delight Me / Vampire / Do It / Bite Me / Excite Me."

When he finished, Helenska and Gertrude were both weeping. Their faces and collarbones were bright red and flushed, and their eyes were glassy. The men were all staring down at their feet and muttering and frowning. Lucas Smith looked as though he were going to choke on his cigar.

I stood up and clapped politely, surprised by what an old-fashioned poet Byron Ravage had turned out to be. Then, without looking at anyone, including Byron Ravage, I climbed those steep stairs to my bedroom. I got into my white nightgown, I lay in bed, and I began reading my own work aloud. But for the first time ever, I felt restless, as though I needed more than the sound of my own voice to turn me on. I didn't fall asleep until well past midnight. And instead of dreaming about jocks in the locker room, I dreamed about vampire lovers in long black capes who made wild love to me on the tops of Ping-Pong tables.

In the morning, I was amazed at the effect that Byron Ravage's poem had had on me. I grew more determined than ever to avoid him, and to concentrate exclusively on my work for the language committee. In fact, I decided what I would do next would be to invent a new name for Ping-Pong. A name that Byron Ravage wouldn't like.

★ ★ ★

A few weeks later, at breakfast, Byron Ravage made two more announcements. First, he said, looking right at me, he'd decided that he wanted to join the language committee. And, second, he said, still looking right at me, he wanted to play Ping-Pong in the evenings.

Well, I thought, I would simply resign from the language committee. No, that would be too obvious. Besides, I'd grown obsessed with trying to come up with a new name for Ping-Pong, a name that would change the meaning of the game forever, but none of the names I'd come up with fit.

But, as it turned out, Byron Ravage was so silent during the language committee meetings that I really had no need to quit. He sat apart from the rest of us, his legs stretched out in front of him. He didn't seem to care a twit about inventing new toys, games, and sports-related items for Game-i-Con. Still, sometimes I had the uneasy sensation that he was watching me.

I did, however, stop playing Ping-Pong. Soon after, I began hearing rumors that the games had changed, that Byron encouraged people to play for money, and that one night he even instigated a "strip" Ping-Pong game.

So I joined the VCR crowd instead. Lucas Smith was more or less in charge of the movie selection. He was a horror movie buff, with a lifelong fascination for vampire movies. Among the films we watched were Bela Lugosi's scary *Dracula,* Andy Warhol's tongue-in-cheek *Dracula,* and Frank Langella's moody *Dracula.* Although I liked Bela's version best, Lucas seemed to prefer Frank Langella's version. He took copious notes while he watched it. But it was much too dreamy and romantic for my taste. Also, I didn't like the fact that Miss Lucy was still madly in love with Dracula at the end. That just didn't seem right. Naturally, whenever I watched those bloodsucking Count Draculas on the VCR screen, I couldn't help but think of Byron Ravage, and of the poem he'd read to us, and of the way he'd looked at me that night by the fireplace. Not that I believed that Byron Ravage was a vampire. What I believed was this: just as the collective unconscious was filled with our sexual fantasies, it was filled, too, with our fantasies about monsters and demons. I simply wondered what it was in Byron Ravage's particular psychological makeup that had inspired him to write a poem about two vampire lovers. That was all.

Then, one night, Helenska and Gertrude, who had both joined the Ping-Pong crowd after Byron began playing, appeared in the doorway of the VCR room. They stood there silently for a moment, staring right at me. We were watching a humorous film that night, about a bunch of rich, snotty teenagers in L.A. who became vampires. I was in a pretty good mood, because just that morning, I'd come up with what I thought was a halfway decent name for volleyball: smash.

"Rowena, come downstairs and play Ping-Pong with us," Gertrude said imperiously, touching the shimmering pearls around her neck.

"Byron wants to play with you, Rowena," Helenska added in a shaky voice. I remembered hearing some rumors that she'd recently been ill.

"Yes, he requested *you*, Rowena, specifically." Gertrude's voice was unfriendly.

Lucas Smith was staring intensely at me, as though the decision I was about to make—whether or not to play Ping-Pong with Byron Ravage—was the most momentous decision I would ever make in my entire life. Although I didn't want to play, I also didn't think there was any reason for Lucas to stare at me like that. He was annoying me so much that I said, "Sure, I'll play." Lucas fingered his cross and turned away from me. But before he turned away, I saw both sorrow and anger in his eyes.

I closed the door to the VCR room behind me, and I followed Helenska and Gertrude down the stairs to the basement. Helenska, who was wearing a garish green gown and golden pumps on her feet, really did look ill. She was pale, and her hands shook. I remembered more details from the recent rumors about her: she'd been playing much too much Ping-Pong with Byron Ravage; she'd been running a fever; she had no appetite; she experienced mysterious, asthmalike attacks during which she gasped desperately for air.

When I got downstairs, Byron was standing in an arrogant pose, leaning his bony hip against the corner of the Ping-Pong table. He smiled at me with those thin, mean-looking lips.

"I want you to know, Mr. Ravage," I said, "that I'm not interested in playing for money, or in stripping."

"Ah, Rowena Ardsley," he said, in a humble voice, "how you misread my intentions. I simply want to play a good game of Ping-Pong with you."

Helenska and Gertrude stood together at the side of the

table, watching us. They looked at Byron with adoration. They looked at me with distrust. Helenska appeared to be growing weaker and weaker.

The game began. Immediately, it became apparent that not only would I lose, but that I would lose without scoring a single point. Byron was the King of Ping-Pong. He was merciless. He played like a savage, like a man possessed. His mirrored sunglasses glittered. He was everywhere. He was a wall, returning my every shot. He was a military strategist, playing to all my weaknesses, forcing me to run around the table in a way I'd never run before. He smashed the ball so hard it ricocheted around the room. When he put spin on the ball, it spun so fast it became nearly invisible. He smiled cruelly each time he scored a point. He insisted on playing game after game with me. And I had no will to resist him.

At around eleven o'clock, Helenska felt too ill to remain downstairs in the musty Ping-Pong room. She asked Gertrude to help her climb those steep stairs to the second floor. Although Gertrude gave Byron one final glance of regret, she agreed to help Helenska. They'd developed some sort of sisterly bond, it seemed, in their shared lust for Byron Ravage.

And then I was alone with him, with no audience. And no one to protect me, either, I realized. I was sweating and flushed.

Slowly, with great deliberation, he walked toward me, holding his paddle in his hand. I wondered if he were going to hit me with it. Instead, he laid it down very gently on the tabletop, and he placed his hands on my shoulders. His sunglasses were glowing. I wanted to look away from him, to break free of what I knew was the riveting gaze behind those glasses. But I couldn't. "I've been waiting for you for a long, long time, Rowena Ardsley," he said. "Longer than you can imagine. You are special. You are the one I've wanted.

Helenska," he spat out the name, "is nothing to me. I will suck her dry of her essence and then simply turn her into one of the ordinary Undead. Women like Helenska are a dime a dozen, easily seduced, easily bitten, easily discarded. And when I'm through with Helenska, perhaps I'll move on to Gertrude. And then to the others." He smiled. "It's true, I'm a bit of a compulsive biter, but I've really had no choice. It's been all about survival. Nevertheless," he said, seductively, eyeing first my breasts, and then my neck, "I know that you, Rowena Ardsley — dreamer of jockstraps and garter belts, semiotician of the locker room — are unique. And so you shall be my equal, my match. I shall not dominate you, except when we both want me to, of course. And you shall not dominate me, except when we both want you to. In other words, as a species apart, we are free to defy all the old, standard, boring formulas for love and romance. Do you understand?" He waited for my response.

Well, I ask you, what's a girl to do at a moment like that? Because suddenly I believed both in vampires and true love. I nodded my head.

"Then it's settled," he said. "I claim you, Rowena Ardsley. You and I shall play Ping-Pong together for all the centuries to come."

And, before I could do or say a thing, he leaned forward and sank his sharp teeth into my neck. And I would be lying to you if I said that, even for one second, I tried to resist.

★ ★ ★

I don't remember much about the next few days after that. I spent them in a delirious, feverish haze. I do remember, though, that I lay drenched in sweat on my bed, wearing only my flimsy white nightgown, and that I kept dreaming about making love to Byron Ravage on top of the institute's Ping-

Pong table. In my dreams I wore nothing but a black garter belt, and he wore nothing but a long black cape.

I also remember that, at one point, Helenska entered my room and stood over me, her face a ghastly white, her teeth sharpened to fanglike points, with fresh, thick blood dripping from her mouth. And I remember her saying, "Why did he choose you, Rowena Ardsley, to be his vampire lover, to play eternal Ping-Pong with, while I've been condemned to the endless life of the mainstream, the banal Undead? I hate you, Rowena Ardsley!" And then she was gone — poor, pathetic creature of the night that she'd become — and I fell back to sleep.

I also remember, at some point, all of the men at the institute, including the CEO of Game-i-Con, standing over my bedside, too, all muttering something about saving me, and vengeance, and male bonding, and how it was their duty to rid the world once and for all of the inhuman beast in human form. Their voices were loud and angry, and it seemed to me, in my feverish haze, that not only Lucas Smith, but all of them, were wearing crosses around their necks, and that they had strung wreaths of garlic around their waists. The smell of all that garlic made me feel even sicker.

Finally, after I don't know how many hours or days or weeks, the fever passed. I felt fine. I felt, in fact, like a brand-new woman, as though I had been reborn. I was no longer the same Rowena Ardsley. And what I wanted at that moment, more than anything in the world, was to be with Byron Ravage, to be in his arms, to make fierce love to him.

I rose, turned on the light, and looked at myself in the small, oval mirror over my bureau. What I saw was this: red eyes, pointy teeth, chalk-white skin. I looked absolutely ravishing! But the light hurt my eyes, so I shut it off. I wasn't even slightly surprised that I could see clearly in the dark.

Still wearing my flimsy nightgown, I slipped out of my bedroom. I headed directly down the long dark corridor that led to Byron's bedroom. I opened his door. Although his room was dark, I saw him clearly, and I know he saw me clearly, too, as I stood there in his doorway. He lay in his bed, on top of the covers, with his head propped up against the wooden headboard. He wasn't wearing his mirrored sunglasses. For the very first time I saw his eyes. Like mine, they were red. And, like mine, they burned with passion.

I entered his room, closing the door behind me. I walked to his bed. I stood over him.

"Ah, Rowena Ardsley," he said, "now you are almost ready. I need to bite you just one more time. For you are halfway there, halfway transformed. You are half woman, and half creature of the night. Which means that you are only half mine. But if you will just lie here beside me, my darling, I shall fully transform you, to turn you into my Queen of the Night, into my Queen of Ping-Pong. You shall be my eternal, garter belt–wearing, Ping-Pong–playing bride!"

Obediently, I sank down beside him, ready to join him for all eternity. It was the most erotic — the most sensual — moment of my life. He reached out for me, and I offered him my neck. But just then, the door to his room was flung open, and all of the men of the institute burst in, shouting wild obscenities. The nauseating smell of garlic accompanied them. They carried flaming torches, and weapons of all sorts: knives, pistols, machetes, rifles, and silver daggers. The men of the institute had become a lynch mob.

I screamed, but my screams were useless. They grabbed Byron, and they threw a green Ping-Pong net around his neck, pulling it so tightly he couldn't breathe. They stood over him, twisting the net tighter and tighter, and then they took the ends of it, and they pinned down his arms. Lucas

Smith was clearly the head of the group, the ringleader. At last I understood why he'd taken such copious notes during Frank Langella's *Dracula*. He'd been noting how, in the movie, the vampire hunters had captured Dracula in a big fishing net. And, Byron, like Frank Langella, writhed and struggled, trying to break free. Then he moaned aloud. It was a heartbreaking moan, filled with agony and bewilderment and rage. But there was absolutely nothing that I, who loved him so, could do to help him.

Byron, caught in that net, began to turn ancient before my eyes. He was transformed into the oldest creature on this planet. He grew hideous and mottled and grotesque. And, as he grew old and frail, as his life ebbed, I could feel myself growing wholly human again. I could feel the blush returning to my cheeks, and the points vanishing from my teeth. The red glow of the world — my new fiery vision — was fading. I was miserable. I didn't want to go back to being Rowena Ardsley, semiotician of the locker room, dreamer of sexual submission to brawny jocks. I wanted, more than anything in the world, to be a vampire. I wanted to play Ping-Pong with Byron Ravage for all the centuries to come. I wept and wept.

"Hoorah!" I heard Lucas Smith shout. "We may have lost Helenska, but we've saved Rowena!" Perhaps he thought my tears were tears of gratitude. "Hoorah!" all of the other men shouted, and then, congratulating each other, they slapped one another on the back. They had the same kind of excited camaraderie among themselves that the jocks in my dreams always had. Turning their backs on Byron, they all stared at me. And I saw pure savagery on their faces, and I knew what was going through their minds. They wanted to take me at that very moment, to have their brutal way with me. I felt unable to breathe. I felt claustrophobic. At that moment, there were just too many damned sexual fantasies crowding that one small, dark bedroom. Too much damned collective unconscious all around. And I didn't want those men to rape me. But then I saw Lucas Smith fingering the cross on his neck, and I knew that he would resist the temptation, and that all the other men would follow his lead. I was saved. I could breathe again.

And that was the very same moment, when their backs were turned to Byron and they were wrestling with temptation, that I saw it, what none of the rest of them saw: the sleek black bat that freed itself effortlessly from the Ping-Pong net and flew gracefully and swiftly out the window.

★ ★ ★

Five years have passed since that night. I have no doubt, no doubt at all, that Byron Ravage is very much alive. Somewhere, he gains strength for his triumphant return. The King of the Vampires, the King of the Ping-Pong table, has not been vanquished. All other men pale in comparison to him. And I don't feel at all like a victim, you must understand. I've *chosen* this fantasy, after all. I've chosen to love a vampire.

Meanwhile, I've returned to the university. Game-i-Con went out of business, and the institute was destroyed a few months later in a mysterious fire. I do hear bits of news now and then about the other members of the institute, though. I heard, for instance, that Lucas Smith drove his car off a cliff one day, and that he didn't even leave a suicide note behind. And that the CEO, who'd become destitute, had taken a deliberate overdose of drugs. And I know, of course, without being told, what Helenska is doing. She's out haunting a graveyard somewhere under cover of the night.

And, although I continue to teach and to write books, my

scholarly reputation is waning. Instead of being considered a writer of brilliant, if rather obscure, tracts about sports, I'm now thought of as a wild-eyed eccentric because now I write exclusively about Ping-Pong. Eventually, I suspect, I'll have drawers full of unpublished manuscripts. But I don't really mind. I've dedicated myself, body and soul, to decoding the hidden language of the game's slams, spins, and strategies. Because it *is* Ping-Pong, I've come to see, that is the chosen game, the game that glows with the eternal fire, the game that, ultimately, will entice Byron Ravage to rise up from his long sleep beneath the earth, to walk once more among human beings. It's more subtle than other games. A brainy game, not a brawny game. Sure, it's not for everyone. But I refuse to apologize if Ping-Pong is only understood by the select few who can discern its erotic nature.

So I keep myself busy while I wait for Byron to return to me. In addition to my writing, I collect sexy black garter belts, which I keep in a trunk beneath my bed. Oh, and by the way, I've finally come up with a new name for the old game of Ping-Pong. A name that I think will please even Byron, whom, of course, I no longer wish to offend. The name that fits the game like a sleek black glove is Vampire Ball. I'm sure you agree.

★ ★ ★

Ladies with Long Hair

(In memory of Robert)

WE — THE LADIES WITH LONG HAIR, all dressed in black — are here for our meeting.

I'm wearing a black jersey turtleneck, black jeans, black leather jacket, and black pointed cowboy boots. I feel tough, ready to do battle, whether it's on the mean streets of New York City, or in the open spaces of the Wild West.

We're meeting in a hotel auditorium in midtown Manhattan. The hotel is part of a national chain. The auditorium, bland and generic, encourages anonymity. But we, the ladies with long hair, refuse such anonymity. We want to be noticed. We *insist* on being noticed.

There are about a hundred of us. A woman named Jennifer is scheduled to begin the meeting. Jennifer, in her early twenties, walks onto the stage. "Testing, testing," she says into the mike. Her voice is high-pitched. She's pretty in a schoolgirl way, with freckles and very long, very bright, red hair. She's wearing a black jersey miniskirt, black, slouchy socks, and a black knit shirt with black lace on the collar. Jennifer reads from our rulebook:

> *We, the ladies with long hair, resolve always to wear black, and never to cut our hair until a cure for the plague has been found. We resolve to do everything within our power to ensure that enough money, time, and effort go into finding a cure for the plague, and to ensure that those who are now sick receive the best care possible. With our long, long hair and our black, black clothes, we shall serve as a living, breathing, walking, talking conscience for a nation that has misplaced its own.*

Jennifer finishes to loud applause. Shyly ducking her head, she joins the rest of us out in the audience. I feel tears on my face. The other women are crying, too. We cry every month at our meetings. I take a strand of my long, thick, wavy, chestnut-colored hair, and twist it tightly around my fingers as I weep.

Mallory, about fifty, strides onto the stage. She's one of the original founders of our group. Her long, black cotton dress brushes the floor of the stage. Her frizzy salt-and-pepper hair falls way past her waist. She adjusts her black-framed eyeglasses. She clears her throat, and begins to speak. "Thank you, Jennifer," she says, "and thank you, ladies, for coming today." Her voice is clear and strong. "Now, onto the next part of our meeting—the testimonials."

I wipe my eyes and blow my nose. Many of us raise our hands. Mallory calls on us one by one, and we rise and take our turns at the podium.

"He made me feel like a princess"—a woman in a wheelchair is speaking. She's been helped to the stage by two other women. Her silky blond hair is tied into two long braids, which are woven through with black ribbons. "I've been in a wheelchair since I was a kid," she says. Her voice is soft. "People—even my own sister and brother—are embarrassed by me. But Billy always made me feel special. Billy curled my hair, waved it, dyed it. He indulged my fantasies, never finding it comical that I wanted to look glamorous. So I wear my black ribbons for Billy, who was my age, twenty-two."

"Jean-Paul asked after my kids, remembered that Mark, who's in the fifth grade, has problems reading, and Jeanette, who's sixteen, didn't have a boyfriend." The next speaker is about thirty-five, a brisk lawyer type, with long dark hair held in place by a shiny black barrette. She's wearing a black suit, and carrying a black leather attaché case. "My closest friends talk to me about business and money — they *never* remember to ask after my kids. They never even remember I *have* kids. But Jean-Paul never forgot a thing I told him."

"Charlie was weeping one afternoon, so I got up from the chair with my hair sopping wet and a towel over my shoulders, and I held him, while he told me about the pain of growing up feeling ashamed and different, and how, finally, when he moved to San Francisco, he saw that he wasn't alone." The woman speaking is wearing black dungaree overalls and black sandals with thick, rippled soles. Her silvery hair, parted on the side, falls to her collarbone. She's probably a longtime feminist, I think, one of those who marched back in the seventies, when I was still a naive teenager dreaming about growing up and living in a penthouse, owning a yacht, and dating wealthy, handsome businessmen.

"I've had plenty of hairdressers, nasty little shits who see us as objects, you know," says a fortyish woman with thick black eye makeup and furry black false eyelashes. She's wearing a black velour pantsuit, and black rhinestone-studded high heels. She's not the kind of person I would have been drawn to, before. But now, I feel like her kin. "But Miguel would look at *you*," she goes on, batting her eyes, "at *your* particular bone structure, and whether you wore round earrings or dangling ones. Miguel would ask whether you enjoyed spending hours and hours in the morning with curlers and hairpins, as I confess I do," she laughs, breathlessly, "or whether you can't bear to fuss with your hair. Oh, Miguel," her voice breaks, "I miss you so much." She leaves the stage, head down.

"Neddie was such fun! I laughed more there, in his chair, than anywhere else. Sometimes he would do what he called his 'queenie number,' bitching and camping it up and gossiping and we would laugh until there were tears in our eyes." A very short, perky woman with long pigtails, wearing a black stirrup catsuit and black ankle boots, wipes her blue eyes as she speaks. I smile, imagining her and Neddie having a ball, exchanging their gossipy, bitchy tidbits.

"Larry grew up in the Bronx. He was a Red Diaper baby, like me," a woman with one long braid down her back, announces. She's a college professor, I decide, serious and scholarly. I picture her sitting in Larry's chair and, as he snipped, the two of them discussing the imminent working-class revolution, feeling less alone in their beliefs because they had each other.

At last it's my turn. I look forward to this moment every month, to my chance to talk about Chris. I'm not at all frightened of standing on stage, of addressing such a large audience. "Chris was the kindest, most generous person I ever knew," I say. And I talk about how hard he worked, how he scrimped and saved to open his own SoHo salon, how he loved to jog in Washington Square Park late at night, how he loved to splurge and go to New Age spas and do aromatherapy and herbal massage, how he always listened to me, whether I was feeling up or down, and how he was always honest and direct with me, never holding back his deepest emotions. I talk about how his grandmother was the only one in his family who hadn't cut him off when he moved to New York and became a hairdresser.

When we've finished our testimonials, there's not a dry eye in the auditorium. The elderly woman next to me, whose white hair is pinned up into a thick bun with old-fashioned metal hairpins, tells me she's flown in from Miami for this meeting. "For twenty years, once a week, I saw Samuel, and he did everything for me — dyed, cut, combed, taught me how to roll a bun, a French twist. . . . We went out together to concerts, things my friends didn't want to go to — the Pointer Sisters," she says, "and Billy Joel." She holds my hand briefly. Diamond rings glitter on her fingers. "Once a week for twenty years. My own children don't speak to me once a week."

Mallory is back on stage, calling on us one by one to discuss what we've been doing since our last meeting. A Las Vegas woman organized a rally outside a church. A performance artist was arrested at Columbus Circle for stripping to her underwear and singing an angry song about the plague, and is out on bail. A Mormon in Salt Lake City launched a letter-writing campaign. The elementary school–age daughters of a social worker are letting their hair grow out in solidarity. I talk about how I stood before a group of local politicians, aggressively pointing to charts and slides, aggressively quoting facts and figures, to show them that they're not doing enough, and to remind them that they and their loved ones could be next, that one needn't be a hairdresser to be struck down, and that, besides, anyone — *anyone!* — can grow up and become a hairdresser, even their own daughters, even their own sons.

When we're finished, a skinny woman wearing a sleeve-less, tight, black shift rises from the audience and walks to the podium. Her wild brown hair comes almost to her knees. Her expression is angry, her voice defiant. "I've been alone for five years since a *very* ugly divorce," she says. "I'm a cabaret singer, and I haven't been able to find work. I've been severely depressed. Finally — *finally!* — I've met a man. And he's handsome. And rich. But," her voice grows even more defiant, "he doesn't like my hair this long. He doesn't find it flattering. He wants me to cut it." She looks at us with an expression I can't read — pride or despair, I'm not sure which. She goes on, continuing to speak angrily about her dilemma, but now I'm thinking about my own boyfriend, Paul, also rich and handsome, who left me almost as soon as I began to grow my hair long. I no longer looked the way he wanted me to look when we dined out together in restau-rants, when we went to cocktail parties with his colleagues. And I suspect that every woman in the auditorium is thinking, at this moment, of someone she loves — or loved — who objects to her being a lady with long hair.

Whatever we may be thinking, though, none of us inter-rupt the woman on stage. We never try to convince anyone to stay. Sometimes members drop out. I've run into a few of them afterward, on the street, with their hair freshly cropped, curled, and lacquered. They avoid my eyes, turn their heads, walk on at a faster pace. Last week, late at night in a twenty-four-hour supermarket in the West Village, I saw a lady who'd stopped coming to meetings months and months ago. We were both on line to pay. "It's happened to me again," she explained to me, as the other people on line eyed my long hair. "I grew dependent on someone new, at a salon on Broadway, and he was kind, talented, warm, dependable, newly in love, monogamous with a wonderful person," her voice grew soft and sad, "and then he was struck by the plague and then he died. So I'm going to rejoin the ladies with long hair. I *have* to."

I hugged her right there at the cash register. I looked into her eyes. "I'm so sorry," I said, "so very sorry." I held her tightly. "But I'm glad you've returned to us. It's the right thing to do." She hugged me back, and then we paid for our groceries. "Your hair will look so beautiful, again," I added.

The skinny woman in the black shift is leaving the stage, still angry, still defiant, still confused. The elderly woman next to me whispers, "She'll stay with us, I can tell." One of her hairpins falls into my lap. I hand it back to her. "She'll stay," she repeats, reinserting the metal hairpin into her bun.

Mallory takes the stage again. She gives us the information about our next meeting, to be held at a theater down in North Carolina. "Until next month, ladies," she says, "work hard."

And we, the ladies with long hair, rise from our seats. We file out of the auditorium, and through the hotel lobby, where a group of Japanese tourists takes our picture, and a man in a fatigue jacket shakes our hands, and a little girl points and says, excitedly, "Look, Mommy, ladies with long hair!" while her short-haired mother waves at us.

The air outside the hotel is brisk. I watch as some of us gather together in groups and hail taxis, and some of us walk off alone in various directions, uptown and downtown, East Side and West Side. I take a few deep breaths, cross the street, and head down the dark, narrow stairs leading to the subway, feeling fast and sure, in my black jeans, black leather jacket, and black cowboy boots, with my long, thick, wavy, chestnut-colored hair flying out behind me.

★ ★ ★

Aunt Lulu, The Condom Lady, Dispenses Advice

Dear Aunt Lulu:

I am an up-and-coming, young, beautiful, socially conscious, female actor (note the term *female actor,* as opposed to the demeaning act*ress,* or worse yet, *starlet!*) who is *sure* to be nominated for an Oscar this year for my lead role in that sparkling, romantic, action-comedy set in New York, Cleveland, and Istanbul (no names, but does the line, "When I look into your baby blues, I see my life passing before my eyes?" mean anything to you?). But here's the rub: I would like to make a major fashion-*plus*-social statement at the Oscars! But how? What shall I wear to distinguish myself, to stand out from the crowd? (Of course, I've been approached by all the top designers, but I'd rather die than look like another size-four, Hollywood clone!) Please, you must help me, Aunt Lulu! My career is in your hands!

— *Signed,*

Politically Correct, & Pretty Too, in Malibu

Dear Politically Correct, & Pretty Too, in Malibu:

Do you remember that stunning dress composed exclusively of gold American Express cards worn at the Oscars a few years back? Well, *you'll* stand out in a dress stitched together with condoms! Nothing but condoms! Day-glo condoms, designer condoms, lamb's wool, basic, etc.! You'll be the talk of Hollywood, of the entire world! And, my dear, you'll make a *major* statement for Condom Power! But do be careful to keep in mind Aunt Lulu's personal motto that night whenever you get up, sit down, pose for the paparazzi, or make any sudden moves: **WEAR ONE, DON'T TEAR ONE!**

Dear Aunt Lulu:

My boyfriend plays guitar and writes the most lyrical, sensitive songs you can imagine. He looks like a cross between Eddie Vedder and Vincent van Gogh. But I have a problem. He doesn't want to use a condom. We've reached, like, an impasse. What shall I do?

— *Signed,*

Condom-Rattled in Seattle

Dear Condom-Rattled in Seattle:

A cross between Eddie Vedder and Vincent Van Gogh? He wears flannel shirts, has a red beard, and is missing an ear? I know the type. Dump him! You'd be better off with a cross between Bela Lugosi and Charles Laughton, or Mr. Ed and Frances the Talking Mule, as long as he wears one. But whatever your new, grungy boyfriend looks like, give him this tip from Aunt Lulu: **WEAR ONE, DON'T TEAR ONE!**

Dear Aunt Lulu:

I'm a virile, old-fashioned kind of guy. I grew up down south, in Mississippi, where Elvis comes from. Heck, the ladies tell me I look like Elvis! Back then, when I was growing up, condoms were "dirty." We used them with the bad girls in the backseats of cars. Girls with names like Jezebel and Scarlett. We didn't use them with the nice girls. We married the nice girls, had children with the nice girls. Well, my nice girl took the children and ran off with the local optometrist, a nice boy. So now I'm here in Tupelo, divorced and back on the old Date-o-Rama. Don't get me wrong. It's not so bad. I'm dating a mighty sweet, college-educated gal. But Aunt Lulu, she carries condoms in her purse, I swear, and she even . . . *likes* . . . using them! Heck, when she whips out a condom from her pretty, little, silk purse, I feel sordid and bad, like I'm with Jezebel or Scarlett in the backseat of my daddy's car. What's a good old boy to do?

Signed —

Elvis Is Blue in Tupelo

Dear Elvis Is Blue in Tupelo:

Sordid and bad is good! It's the American Way! Squeaky clean and vanilla is bad! Keep dating that sweet, college-educated gal with the latex in her pretty purse! She knows *exactly* what she's doing. Lucky you! And next time she's opening the wrapper with her teeth why don't you lean over and whisper in her pretty little ear, in your deepest, sexiest Elvis drawl: **HECK, HONEY, WEAR ONE, DON'T TEAR ONE!**

Confidential to Little Billy Peck in Teaneck:

No, Little Billy Peck, wearing a condom will not make you any taller! Big Billy Peck, your older brother in Teaneck, is pulling your leg. But if you *don't* wear one, you'll end up with hairy palms, and when you die you'll go to the Bad Place! Trust me, Little Billy Peck in Teaneck! **WEAR ONE, DON'T TEAR ONE!**

And now a final note to all my dear, turned-on, latex-needy readers: Please don't hesitate — not for a nanosecond! — to send your condom questions to Aunt Lulu, the Condom Lady, by snail mail, fax, or e-mail. And be sure to check out Rubber Chat, *Aunt Lulu's brand-new site on the Internet. Use it Now! Toodle-oo!*

A Spy in the Land of the Ladies Who Lunch

I T WASN'T LIKE I ASKED FOR THIS assignment. I vastly would have preferred to infiltrate some multinational corporation, or the staff of some crackpot neo-Nazi political candidate. But instead, the leader of my revolutionary group assigned me this territory: Fifth Avenue, the land of the ladies who lunch; the ladies with big hats, facelifts, and tummy tucks; the ladies who preside so magnificently over those endless charity balls. In other words, *you're* my assignment, Samantha.

Luckily, my revolutionary group keeps me well-supplied with cash, donated from sympathizers overseas. That way, I can shop with you at Bergdorf's, and be massaged side by side with you at the spa, and, of course, have lunch with you at *chic* eateries, like we're doing right now. And all the while, I'm spying on you.

Yes, even now, I'm spying, Samantha, as you complain to me one more time about your philandering, millionaire husband, and your spoiled son and daughter who take your money but neither love nor respect you. Yes, I'm spying, Samantha, as you whine about the fact that because you're not as beautiful as you once were, it's only your vast amount of money that keeps you from being nothing in the eyes of the world.

As always, I offer you my sympathy. And, as always, you grow more and more sorry for yourself, and more and more inebriated, until soon you'll begin to spill the beans. You'll start revealing incriminating details about the ways in which you and your husband oppress the rest of us. And those drunkenly-delivered details are precisely what my revolutionary group needs in order to plan our strategy — all of which reminds me, it's time for a drink.

Darling Samantha, let's have some sherry for starters. I know how much you love sherry!

Poor, poor Samantha, always fighting and losing your battles with your various addictions: liquor, cigarettes, food, pills. First, you down the contents of your glass in one greedy gulp, and now you're going on and on about how I'm more like a daughter to you than your own bratty flesh-and-blood bitchette, she of the debutante balls and the coke habit. I try to smile and appear moved. But, really, honey, there's no need to belabor the point, because that's the whole idea here — for me to make you love and trust me. That's my *modus operandi*.

And I'm damned good at what I do. Although I worry constantly about slipping up. I never answer to my real name, never utter one truthful syllable, never let my guard down for an instant. That's why I get so tired, so weary, even though I'm so much younger than you, who've never worked a day in your life. But it takes its toll, this double life, this running back and forth, from Bergdorf's to the Bronx. That's right— the Bronx, where my revolutionary group meets very, very late at night, in the basement of Building Number Four in the projects, where I was born and bred. It's true, darling, I've lied to you all along: my mother is no European countess, my father no international diplomat. I wasn't educated abroad. My education comes from the streets. But how could you guess? I play my part so well.

Yes, darling Samantha, the sherry is nice and dry. What's that? You're hungry? But of course, how silly of me! Let's order!

I should recognize your hunger by now. After all, I've seen it many times, that hungry, yearning, desperate look in your false-eyelashed, unblinking eyes — unblinking, of course, because of all the facelifts.

Oh, you'd like to share an appetizer first? Certainly, darling, your wish is my command. Which one? The shrimp cocktail? The stuffed mushrooms? Fine, fine! Garçon, we'll have both. And of course, darling, you're absolutely right, more sherry!

Damn, this sherry is making me sleepy. So sleepy. But I can't let you see that, Samantha. I must look chipper, perky, ever-alert to you and your whims.

My, the shrimp cocktail is superb. Do have more, darling Samantha!

Now, now, there's no need for you to act coy with me, to pretend you don't want any more. I know how enormous your appetite is.

What's that, Samantha? You want to move on to the harder stuff? Fine, fine! Garcon, two vodka martinis straight up! Oh, and darling Samantha, don't forget, there's also hot, fresh bread on the table, and lush, creamy butter!

I do take some wicked pleasure, I confess, in watching you eat, when I know you're so worried about waking up one morning with an extra ounce of flesh on you. While I, on the other hand, never need to worry about my weight. Class rage is all I need to keep me thin. Not a rich girl's frail kind of thin, either, but a poor girl's thin: mean and lean. I've got to be tight and wiry, ready to fight the class war, and ready to defend myself to the death should I be discovered.

But, of course, darling Samantha, what fun, let's do order second martinis, and let's do make them doubles!

Now, now, I see you're starting to smile — although didn't you tell me it hurts when you smile because of the collagen shots? Well, in any case, it's nice that you're laughing, that you've entered that drunken state where everything seems humorous to you. It's good to have a sense of humor. My sense of humor is one of my weapons in your world. All spies need a sense of humor. Some of my brothers and sisters in the revolutionary group never, never laugh, you see. They tell me they just can't find anything funny about poverty. They're right, of course: the revolution ain't no joke. When I ride the subway up to the Bronx late at night, I'm not laughing; and when we plan your demise deep in the basement of Building Number Four, I'm not laughing then, either.

Darling, you seem somewhat restless. What's the matter? Oh, you want to go to the Little Girl's Room to powder your nose?

Give me a break — you're really going to shove two

skinny, gnarled, impeccably manicured fingers down your cigarette-scarred throat to make yourself throw up. Go ahead. Just be quick about it. I don't like letting you out of my sight for too long. I know your neurotic, narcissistic, bulemic routine — while there are people starving all over the world, all over this city. But you don't want to hear about those others who have so much less than you. It's not your problem, darling. Of course not. You do what you can — all those dull charity events. . . .

Ah, you're back, darling. I've ordered some more bread for us. And butter, butter, butter!

Anyway, Samantha, here's the bottom line — I would love to see you bleed, right here, all over the linen tablecloth, all over your silk *Chanel* suit, right here, in this *chic* little eatery, all over this most obliging waiter, who keeps bringing us more bread, more butter, more vodka martinis. . . .

It isn't that you haven't been nice to me. You have, in your own self-centered, two-faced way. I'd be the first to admit it. But, you see, because my mother died ill and haggard and destitute, I've never really been able to "bond" with you, as the psychologists say — I mean, not really, not deep, deep down. I confess that I hold a grudge simply because my own mother never had access to spas and plastic surgeons; never had a facial or a massage, a pedicure or a bikini wax; never had the luxury to complain about her acupuncturist and her aromatherapist. My mother worked in a factory, and rode the subway for over an hour twice a day during rush hour, where she had to stand, packed into the hot car with hundreds of strangers, and where she was poked and jabbed and stepped on and fondled; and she grew more and more crippled with arthritis and her fingers ached and ached, and her factory foreman screamed at her and called her lazy and threatened to fire her because her fingers weren't as fast as they used to be, and finally she died, exhausted and old before her time. . . .

No, no, I'm alright. . . . Just ignore me, I know I'm crying, darling Samantha, but martinis always make me melancholy. That's all. Why don't we order our entrées? There, see, I'm better now! No more tears. I'd love the duck Moulard. And you? The escargot? Good choice! Pierre's escargot is fabulous.

There's no denying that my palate has certainly evolved since my days in the projects. And sometimes I wrap up food from *chic* little eateries like this one, and carry it on the subway up to the Bronx, to my revolutionary group. They just love Pierre's *escargot*. Who wouldn't?

Okay, okay, you've caught me, I admit it, I am still crying into my vodka martini. So what is it you'd like to know — whether something is making me unhappy? No, no, you mustn't worry about me, darling! Far more important is that you be happy, Samantha, my dear, dear friend!

You see, happiness is no big deal to me. We girls from the projects don't expect to be happy. Whereas you ladies who lunch, why, you not only expect it, you believe that you alone deserve it. Although I know, of course, that you're really utterly miserable. So, here's a novel idea: Since your money only seems to bring you more and more unhappiness, why not share the wealth? Pass it around! Redistribute the *moola!* Oh, I know, there's no point in my even suggesting it. You wouldn't like that idea one bit. No, you'll just hold on to your money, and you'll keep on whining your way through life, always bitching, complaining about this and that, spending your money on new clothes and jewels and trips abroad, and running to the surgeon's knife, the latest spa, the latest diet, hoping to stay young forever.

Ah, darling Samantha, do pass that hot bread. There, no more tears, I promise! See, I'm smiling now! Thanks, darling!

I might as well fill up on the bread myself. It's so delicious. We never had bread like this in the Bronx. Besides, I've got to keep up my strength. I've still got so much to do today: After you finish your fifth or sixth vodka martini, we'll head together to Bergdorf's; and then we're off to Muffy's cocktail party, where you'll continue to pack away those vodka martinis; and then, of course, late, late at night, long after you and I have called each other "darling" for the hundredth time today, long after we've smeared our rosy pink lipstick on one another's cheeks while kissing each other goodnight, long, long, after a weary working girl like myself should be fast asleep, I'll ride the Number Two IRT up to the Bronx—and to the revolution.

★ ★ ★

The Art of Forgiveness: A Fable

S HE'D WRITTEN HER FIRST POEM when she was six. Her parents had been so proud, they'd framed it and hung it on the living room wall, directly over the pink-and-silver brocade sofa her mother loved so much. She was an urban little girl who played on the rough-and-tumble streets of the Bronx, and her poem celebrated this world she knew:

> *I love the Bronx, where I play.*
> *It is my home, and it is pretty.*
> *And here I play, in New York City.*

Her teacher read the poem aloud before the rest of the class. "She has a gift," her teacher told her mother during

Open School Week. "Writing like this, about something that deeply matters to her, is a spiritual art. And if she wishes, she can grow up to be a writer — an artist of the spirit."

Later, her mother told her what the teacher had said. She felt proud to know that she had a gift, something special. She worked hard from that moment on, studying the writing of others and practicing her own. She fell in love with the very *idea* of language. She would stand in front of her mirror, repeating over and over her favorite words from the poems of Edgar Allan Poe: "bells, bells, bells" and "nevermore, nevermore!" From *The Wizard of Oz,* she would make a song of the characters' names: "Dorothy, Toto, Glinda, Scarecrow, Tin Man, Auntie Em."

Soon after, though, her parents lost interest in her writing. They had other things on their minds, they told her, and besides, they didn't want to encourage her too much, lest she really decide to *become* a writer, something they feared, because it wasn't a secure, conventional way of life.

Eventually, her parents moved south, to a warmer climate. "We're not getting any younger," they told her. She went away to college, and she grew cool toward them. She didn't invite them to her college graduation, and she didn't visit them. Instead, she moved into a small apartment, downtown in the East Village. A few years later, when her second novel won a major prize, she moved uptown to a fancy building with three doormen and three glittering chandeliers in the lobby. She never thought about her childhood in the Bronx. It was long ago, and far away.

Something was wrong, however: Although she was now successful, she felt angry much of the time. She held onto slights and rebuffs; she nursed grudges. If a friend or a lover said a wrong thing, something that hurt or offended her, well then, her heart would harden toward that person. Inevitably, the person would say a *second* wrong thing. And that would be that. She couldn't bear to be in that person's presence ever again.

Still, despite her anger at so many people, she wasn't lonely. She was very charming — her witty, lush language drew people to her—and so it was easy for her to make new friends and lovers.

Once, a friend called her and said, "I'm sorry I said an unkind thing to you. I was wrong. But I'm not perfect. Can't you forgive me?"

She held her breath, and then answered honestly: "No, I can't."

Her friend hung up the phone then, saying, "Well, perhaps I can't forgive *you*, either, for not caring enough to *try!*"

She'd shrugged her shoulders, and gone out to dinner with some new friends.

A few years later, in the midst of a party which was being thrown for her by her newest, most charming friends, she felt a terrible ache in her chest. The ache began just as her hosts were raising their glasses to toast her splendid new book. She smiled and made a short, witty speech, but the ache wouldn't go away.

Weeks went by — then months — and she lived her life as she always had: She spun her web of words; she made new friends and lovers; she recited her own words on stage for large, enthusiastic audiences. But the ache grew worse and worse, more and more painful.

She found herself dreaming at night about those people who had said such terribly wrong things to her. In one dream, she reached out her hand across a great ocean to a lost lover, but he swam away from her, and the farther away he got, the more desperate she was to reach him. In another, she was trapped in quicksand, screaming for help, while her old friend, the one who'd hung up on her, stood by and watched, an inscrutable expression on her face.

She would waken in the middle of the night, saddened and frightened by these dreams, unable to return to sleep. Finally, she went to see a therapist, an older woman with salt-and-pepper hair, kind eyes behind thick tortoiseshell eyeglasses, and a warm smile. "How can I help you?" the therapist asked, leaning back in her big chair.

She told the therapist about her frightening dreams.

"And?" the therapist asked.

So then she told the therapist about all the terribly wrong things people had said and done to her over the years. The list went on and on: so many slights and rude comments; so many terrible and hurtful moments.

"And?" the therapist asked again, when she'd finished.

"And?" she repeated.

"Your language is enthralling," the therapist said, looking thoughtful. "You weave a spell when you speak. It is an art."

"Oh, yes. I'm a writer, you see. An artist of the spirit."

"And?"

She was silent. She just couldn't imagine what the therapist wanted her to say.

"And where is the other word? Despite your large and impressive vocabulary, you never once used the other word. Like the word "art," this word, too, is spiritual."

"A spiritual word?"

"*Forgive,*" the therapist said. "You never said that you forgave anyone."

"I don't *understand* that word," she explained. "That word is abstract to me. Other people use that word, but I never do. Still," she went on bravely, "I think I *would* like to learn the meaning of that word."

The therapist smiled, even more warmly than before. "We shall work together then, to expand your vocabulary."

For ten years, she saw the therapist. During each session, they discussed that word. It was hard work: Sometimes she shouted out with fury; sometimes she wept; sometimes she felt cold and detached. At other times, she felt hopeful, and thought that perhaps she was growing closer to understanding the meaning of that intangible, elusive word.

Over the course of the ten years, the therapist's salt-and-pepper hair turned completely to salt. And she herself, although still firm and trim, saw signs of her own aging: a line here, a wrinkle there, a grey hair both here *and* there. . . .

Meanwhile, she grew more and more accomplished and well-known. Her artistry was honored with increasingly prestigious awards; the audiences for her stage recitations grew larger; and she wrote and published more than ever.

Then one day, after she'd been traveling for many months to promote her newest book, doing interviews every day, giving stage performances every night, sleeping in strange hotel rooms, sometimes running to catch trains and planes, and other times sitting for long hours in cramped waiting rooms while trains and planes were delayed, she managed to steal an hour to fly back to the city for a session with the therapist.

But before she'd even had a chance to sit down, the therapist said something that struck her as *wrong*. The therapist said, "You look very, very tired, my dear. Perhaps the time has come for you to slow down a bit."

She was shocked. And hurt. And enraged. The therapist, who was supposed to know her better than anyone in the world, who she had trusted more than her friends and lovers, had said something *wrong*. Of course, she couldn't slow down. There was no time to slow down. She would have to end therapy immediately. She took a deep breath, intending to tell her therapist this in no uncertain terms. But instead, she said, "I forgive you. I forgive you for saying that." For a long moment, she couldn't believe her own words, but then she realized that they were true.

The therapist smiled her familiar, warm smile and said, "I'm not sure what I said that was so terrible, but how thrilling it is that you forgive me! I'm so happy for you. So very, very happy."

The next morning, she called her therapist and said it again over the phone, adding, "You're right, of course. I am tired. It *is* time for me to slow down."

And then she called her old friend, the same friend who had once said, "Can't you forgive me?" And she said, "I forgive you now. And I understand that I, too, have said many, many wrong things over the years." She paused. "I've missed you so much."

And her friend said, "I've missed you, too. I thought about calling you, but I figured, what was the point, if you didn't even know the one word you needed to know."

"I know, I *know*," she said to her friend, and they laughed like two schoolgirls, and made a lunch date for the very next day.

She spent the rest of the day making calls to old friends and old lovers, to say that she forgave them, and to ask for their forgiveness, as well. And in nearly every case, she was, herself, forgiven. In the few instances where she wasn't, she accepted it, because she was learning, too, that one must accept the consequences of one's actions.

The last call she made was to her parents. Her father had recently had a stroke and was hard of hearing; her mother had arthritis and had trouble walking. As she dialed their number, she pictured them as they once were, so proud, hanging her first poem on the wall above the sofa. To her parents, she didn't say, "I forgive you." She said, instead, "I love you."

By the time she'd finished talking to her parents, the sun had set, and the sky was dark. She turned on the bedroom light, and stood in front of her full-length mirror. She stared at herself—at the lines forming on her face, at the gray hairs here and there, at her firm chin and clear eyes, and she marveled at the power of that one word: "forgive." She repeated it aloud, over and over—the same way she had repeated the words of the poems and stories she'd loved so much as a child —and her body felt more alive than it had in years. She felt once more like that excited, proud little girl who'd written her very first poem celebrating the rough-and-tumble world of the Bronx streets, a world she now vividly remembered. And yet she also felt like a woman growing older and wiser, a woman marching resolutely forward, a woman in touch, at last, with the spirit of the art of forgiveness.

★ ★ ★

Janice Eidus, twice winner of the prestigious O. Henry Prize, is the author of the highly acclaimed *Vito Loves Geraldine,* a collection of stories published by City Lights, and the novels *Urban Bliss* and *Faithful Rebecca.* She lives in New York City, where she was born and raised.